The Abbey Mysteries
The Buried Cross

Other books in the series

The Silent Man
The Scarlet Spring
The Drowned Sword

The Abbey Mysteries

The Buried Cross

Cherith Baldry

OXFORD
UNIVERSITY PRESS

OXFORD

UNIVERSITY PRESS

Great Clarendon Street, Oxford OX2 6DP

Oxford University Press is a department of the University of Oxford.
It furthers the University's objective of excellence in research,
scholarship, and education by publishing worldwide in

Oxford New York

Auckland Bangkok Buenos Aires Cape Town
Chennai Dar es Salaam Delhi Hong Kong Istanbul Karachi
Kolkata Kuala Lumpur Madrid Melbourne Mexico City Mumbai
Nairobi São Paulo Shanghai Taipei Tokyo Toronto

Oxford is a registered trade mark of Oxford University Press
in the UK and in certain other countries

British Library Cataloguing in Publication Data available

ISBN 0 19 275362 2

3 5 7 9 10 8 6 4 2

Printed in Great Britain by
Cox & Wyman Ltd, Reading, Berkshire

Cast of Characters

In the village:

Geoffrey Mason, innkeeper of the Crown in Glastonbury

Idony, his wife

Gwyneth, their daughter

Hereward, their son

Owen Mason, Geoffrey's brother, a stonemason at work on the Abbey

Anne, his wife

Matt Green, a stonemason

Finn Thorson, the local sheriff

Hawisa, his wife

Ivo and Amabel, their twin children, friends of Gwyneth and Hereward

Rhys Freeman, the local shopkeeper

Osbert Teller, his assistant

Tom Smith, the local smith

Hywel, his brother

Dickon Carver, the local carpenter

Margery, his wife
Brigid, their daughter
Mistress Flax, a weaver
Sim Short, a basket-maker
Wat and Hankin, brothers, servants at the Crown

At the Abbey:
Henry de Sully, Abbot of Glastonbury Abbey
Brother Barnabas, the Abbey steward
Brother Padraig, the Abbey infirmarian
Brother Timothy, a young monk
Brother Peter, an old monk
Ralph FitzStephen, sent by King Richard to supervise the rebuilding of the Abbey

Visitors to Glastonbury:
Godfrey de Massard, a priest from Wells Cathedral
Marion le Fevre, an embroideress
Galfridas Hood, her servant
Ursus, a hermit
Wasim Kharab, a merchant
Jack Chapman, a pedlar

Glastonbury, south-west England,
AD 1190

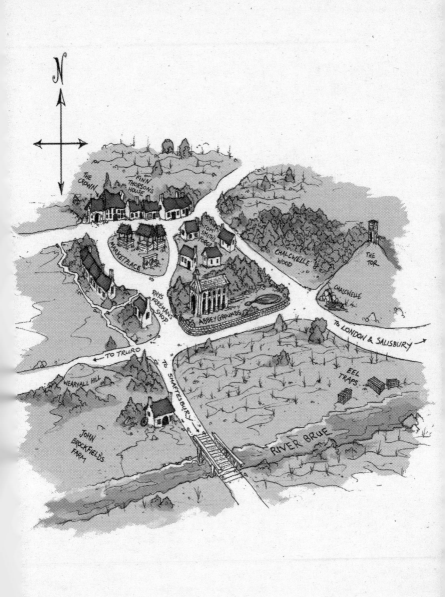

Chapter One

A lost king lies sleeping
Under a green hill . . .

The childish voices drifted along the road which led to Glastonbury Abbey, and thirteen-year-old Gwyneth Mason set down her basket to listen. The old song made her shiver and she gazed up at the Tor, looming through the autumn mist. Here in Glastonbury, living in the shadow of the rounded green hill that rose up like an island from a sea of flat farmland, it wasn't hard to believe that King Arthur lay sleeping there, in a chamber hewn out of the rock.

And lost knights lie with him,
Their swords sleeping still . . .

The voices changed to laughter as the children came running down the road and danced round Gwyneth with their hands linked in a ring.

Gwyneth laughed too, recognizing most of the flushed and scarlet faces. She had helped nurse many a scraped knee and bruised cheek among these babes. Without warning they dropped hands and set off again, skimming along the road like a skein of wild geese, their booted feet scuffling on the mist-damp stones.

A little further behind Gwyneth, her brother Hereward drew into the side of the road to watch them go before trudging on, his stocky figure almost bent double under the weight of two large skins of ale.

'Hurry up,' Gwyneth urged as he came up to her. 'The workmen will be waiting.' She bent down and picked up the large covered basket at her feet. It was so heavy, it might have been stuffed with lumps of iron instead of the bread, cheese, and cold bacon which their father, Geoffrey Mason, sent each day from the Crown Inn to feed the stonemasons who were rebuilding the abbey.

'There's plenty of time,' Hereward replied, soothing his sister as if he was older than her by a twelvemonth instead of the other way round. 'If it was mid-day yet, we would have heard the bell for sext.'

Gwyneth nodded, too breathless to argue. Like everyone in the village, she marked the day in monastic hours, one ear always listening for the chimes that called the monks to their prayers. With Hereward walking beside her, she hauled her basket along the road towards the abbey.

Above the wall, she could just see the roof of the new Lady Chapel, and a corner of the tower that one day would form part of the new church. Six years ago, a terrible fire had destroyed the old abbey. Gwyneth could remember running outside in her nightgown, the stones cold under her bare feet, to hear the shouts of alarm that filled the night and watch the flames leaping into the sky like gigantic orange tongues hungry for stone and wood.

Now there was a new and even more magnificent church rising where the old one had stood. But today, as Gwyneth toiled through the abbey gate, she realized that something was different. Usually at this hour she could hear the pounding of hammers and the clink of chisels on stone, but all was silent. The workmen in their woollen tunics and leather aprons were gathered in groups, looking down towards the gate, or up at the half-built walls. Uneasily, Gwyneth wondered why they were not at work. She shivered as the raw wind whipped her tawny hair across her face and set down her basket to draw her cloak more tightly around her shoulders.

Hereward came up to her, grunting as he shifted his grip on the skins of ale. 'What's going on?'

'I don't know.' Gwyneth frowned. 'Sometimes I think the abbey will never be finished.'

She saw Hereward's mouth tighten. Gwyneth knew that her brother was just as worried as she was. Since the fire, few pilgrims came to the abbey, which meant that fewer people stayed in their father's inn, or bought food and trinkets in the village shops. What would become of the villagers if the abbey was never rebuilt, and the pilgrims never returned?

She was roused from her thoughts by a cheerful shout from the other side of the grassy precinct. A short, stocky man, his black hair streaked with silver like a badger, was hurrying towards them. 'There's Uncle Owen,' Gwyneth said, waving. 'He'll be able to tell us what's going on.'

'Dinner,' Owen Mason greeted them, rubbing his hands with satisfaction. 'That's a welcome sight on a cold day.'

'What's going on?' said Hereward. 'Why is no one working?'

Uncle Owen's expression darkened. 'There's no stone. We were expecting a load to come on barges upriver, but it hasn't arrived.'

'Why not?' Gwyneth asked, as Owen took one of the skins from Hereward and they walked on more slowly towards the church.

Owen shrugged. 'No one knows. Lord Ralph sent a man to find out, but it's my guess the stone hasn't been paid for. So, in the meantime, all we can do is sit here and twiddle our thumbs.' He spread his hands for a moment and looked down at them—broad craftsman's hands, covered with a network of tiny scars where his chisel had nipped at him like a sharp-toothed terrier.

'The king should send more money,' said Hereward. 'Doesn't he want the abbey rebuilt?'

His uncle let out a short bark of laughter. 'All King Richard's money goes to pay for his Crusade in the Holy Land,' he replied. 'He doesn't care what happens here. I heard it said

7

that he would sell London if he could find a buyer.'

That was true, Gwyneth knew. In the first months after the fire, King Henry had provided money to restore the abbey, and even sent his own steward, Ralph FitzStephen, to oversee the work. But since Henry's son Richard had succeeded his father a year ago, the supply of money had dwindled to almost nothing.

The half-finished walls seemed to scowl at Gwyneth as they reached the building site and she began to distribute bread, cheese, and hard bacon to the workmen. Hereward unlaced one of the skins and poured ale into horn beakers. Gwyneth could see from his frown that he was still worrying about the shortage of money to rebuild the abbey.

'Can't Abbot Henry do anything?' he asked, when all the stonemasons had been fed and they were seated with their uncle on a low wall while he ate.

'Maybe,' said Owen, swallowing a mouthful of bread. 'But he's got some other idea in his head just now, though only he and God know what. He had some of our men digging in the graveyard yesterday, and they're at it again today.' He let out a snort, half amused, half disgusted. 'Well, we haven't anything else to do.'

'I hadn't heard that any of the monks had died,' said Gwyneth.

'No more have I.' Owen took a long draught of ale. 'But this isn't a grave they're digging. It's much deeper than that. And Father Abbot gave orders for the place to be curtained off, as if he doesn't want anyone to see inside.'

'Perhaps he knows something is buried there—something that will save the abbey!' Gwyneth exclaimed, her imagination leaping like a fish swimming upstream.

'A chest of treasure, belike.' Her uncle's eyes twinkled with amusement, and Gwyneth felt herself going red.

'Well . . . something!' She sprang to her feet, and tugged Hereward by the sleeve. 'Come on, let's go and see.'

'But they won't let us look,' Hereward reminded her. 'Didn't you hear what Uncle Owen just said?'

'We can try, can't we?' Gwyneth insisted. 'Where are they digging, Uncle Owen?'

'Just outside the Lady Chapel,' Owen told

her. As she set off, dragging a reluctant Hereward with her, he called after them, 'Go careful now. Mind Abbot Henry and Lord Ralph don't catch you spying!'

The Lady Chapel had been the first part of the abbey to be restored, soon after the fire when money was still plentiful. Although the walls had not yet been painted with the colourful scenes from Holy Scripture, the chapel had already been consecrated, and services were held there until the church itself should be ready.

When Gwyneth and Hereward rounded the south-west corner of the chapel, they saw the enclosure their uncle had told them of, made of poles lashed together and covered with curtains of sacking. It had been set up between two ancient stone crosses. A light shone faintly from inside, and Gwyneth could hear voices and movement.

'Keep quiet,' she murmured to Hereward.

Glancing from side to side to make sure no one was watching, she crept across the turf until she stood outside the enclosure. Behind her,

Hereward let out a faint sigh, but still followed. After a moment's careful examination, Gwyneth found the place where the sacking curtains met, and cautiously parted them so that she could peer through. She opened her green eyes very wide. There was little chance of her and Hereward being spotted, that was for sure. The men inside were intent on what they were doing, bent over a hole that yawned darkly in the ground, so deep that Gwyneth could see only the sticky mud-slicked sides, while the bottom lay out of sight.

The turf inside the enclosure had been trampled into slippery mud. A team of workmen and monks, their heavy black robes smeared with earth and kilted to the knee, hauled together on ropes to bring up something from inside the pit. Light from a couple of earthenware lamps shone on faces streaked with sweat and soil.

Abbot Henry himself stood on the opposite side of the pit, his body stooped over like a crow with black-feathered wings folded loosely by its side. There was an expression of intense interest on his thin, scholarly face. Beside him, Ralph FitzStephen, the king's steward, snapped out, 'Have a care! Take up the slack there!'

Gwyneth clutched at the sacking, frustrated that she couldn't see better. If both the abbot and Lord Ralph were supervising the digging, then what was buried in the pit must be really important.

She was aware of Hereward peering over her shoulder and felt his breath warm on her ear as he whispered, 'If we're caught, there'll be trouble.'

Gwyneth impatiently flicked back her hair. 'Hush,' she retorted. 'We won't *be* caught.'

Peering through the gap in the sacking again, she saw that something was rising up to the mouth of the pit. A dark, rounded shape, caked with earth. Gwyneth stared at it for several seconds before she realized it was the trunk of a tree, blackened with age and its long burial.

As the men around the pit heaved on the ropes, it rose waveringly into the light and was guided to rest on solid ground. The workmen relaxed, puffing out their breath and stretching their tired arms.

There was a brief silence as everyone inside the enclosure gazed at the ancient tree trunk. Then Abbot Henry said, 'Take it up. Bring it into the Lady Chapel. No, not you,' he added as two workmen stepped forward. 'Let the monks carry it.'

When several of the monks moved to obey him, Abbot Henry stepped carefully around the pit towards the entrance of the enclosure, fastidiously holding his robes out of the mud that sucked at his sandals. Gwyneth let go her hold on the sacking and dodged around the side, dragging Hereward with her.

'Why would anyone bury a *tree*?' she hissed at him. 'Or bother digging it up? And why does the abbot want it in the Lady Chapel?'

Hereward shrugged, but Gwyneth could see a gleam of interest in his eyes. Her brother's caution, his thoughtful way of speaking, often exasperated her, but she knew he would puzzle away at the problem until he came up with an answer that satisfied him.

Someone inside the enclosure held back the sacking and six monks appeared with the tree trunk supported on their shoulders. Gwyneth felt a shiver run down her spine. They were carrying the long-buried tree as if it were a coffin. The monks paced solemnly towards the Lady Chapel, followed by the abbot and Ralph

FitzStephen. The rest of the monks brought up the rear. Once they had all disappeared inside the chapel, Gwyneth and Hereward hurried across the turf and into the porch.

'I'll wager it's saints' relics,' Hereward murmured, his eyes bright with excitement. 'That would bring the pilgrims back to the abbey, for sure.'

Gwyneth hoped he was right. Every church valued more than anything their sacred relics, traces of far off holy lives like a saint's thigh bone or a scrap of the shroud that Jesus's blessed body had been wrapped in. The belief that touching such artefacts would heal all ills brought pilgrims flocking, from discreetly veiled gentlewomen hoping to cure a pox on their face to the poorest beggars hopping on wooden crutches. But the Glastonbury monks had saved their precious relics of Saint Patrick and the ancient statue of Our Lady from the fire, and not even these had been enough to entice the pilgrims back. This new find would have to be something extraordinary.

Cautiously Gwyneth edged open the door and slid inside the chapel. The tree trunk had been laid in front of the altar on waist-high wooden trestles. Two of the monks had brought torches and stood on either side holding them aloft. The unsteady flames shone brighter by far than the dim autumn light that filtered through the windows.

Abbot Henry and Lord Ralph stood at one end of the tree trunk, while the rest of the monks gathered round. Their faces were stony sombre but their eyes gleamed with a hunger that unnerved Gwyneth and made her weave her fingers for comfort into the edge of her cloak.

Abbot Henry ordered, 'Remove the lid.'

Gwyneth almost exclaimed, 'What lid?' but bit back the words in time. So this wasn't just a tree trunk. It must have been hollowed out to make a chest—or, indeed, a coffin. After all, it had been buried in the graveyard. Perhaps Hereward was right, and it contained the bones of a saint.

There was some fumbling as the monks stooped to do the abbot's bidding, and an impatient hiss from Lord Ralph. Gwyneth shared his impatience. Beckoning to Hereward, she crept further into the chapel until she stood just outside the circle of torchlight. Hereward, at her shoulder, was watching intently; he seemed to have forgotten all his worries about being caught. Besides, all the monks' attention was on the coffin, and no one noticed Gwyneth and her brother hovering in the shadows.

The monks had brought tools from the enclosure but in their inexperienced hands, flitting like pale birds over the rough wooden implements, it took several minutes' levering with iron bars before the coffin lid gave way. Two of the monks lifted it carefully onto the flagstones.

Now Gwyneth could see that the tree trunk had been hollowed out and she craned her neck to make out what was inside, only to find her view blocked by the monks who clustered round it, peering down at the contents.

The abbot answered her curiosity. 'Bones . . .' he said quietly. He and Ralph FitzStephen exchanged a glance. 'Human bones?'

'Yes, Father,' said Brother Padraig, the abbey's infirmarian, a skilled healer who offered his help to the villagers as well as the monks when they fell ill. He stretched one hand into the coffin and pulled out a long, straight bone. 'This here is a shin bone, see?'

'And a marvellous long one,' added Ralph FitzStephen, taking the bone from Brother Padraig. 'Who's the tallest among us?' He snapped his fingers at Brother Timothy, one of the youngest monks, whose gangling figure topped even Abbot Henry. 'Come here.'

His head bowed obediently, Brother Timothy came to stand beside him, and Lord Ralph measured the shin bone against the young monk's leg. 'See,' he said. 'Longer by at least three fingers' breadth. This belonged to a giant of a man!'

Brother Padraig reached into the coffin again and with a steady hand brought out a skull. Gwyneth couldn't help gasping when she saw the empty eye-sockets and the rows of grinning teeth. Returning to his place among the other monks, Brother Timothy glanced towards the muffled sound and narrowed his eyes when he saw the half-hidden shapes.

Gwyneth froze and braced herself for Brother Timothy to alert the abbot to the spies. Instead, the young monk's face creased into a smile and he laid a bony finger on his lips before facing his abbot again.

Limp with relief, Gwyneth returned his

smile. Brother Timothy was the son of the village potter; before he entered the abbey three years ago they had often gone with him on fishing expeditions, or climbed into the abbey orchards in search of apples. It was good to know he still had some loyalty to his childhood friends.

Brother Padraig turned the skull in his fingers. 'There are marks of blows, Father, here . . . and here,' he pointed out to the abbot. 'And look how the skull is splintered. He died of a blow to the head.'

A muted chorus of alarm broke out from among the monks and one of them asked, 'Was he murdered?'

'Not this man,' said Lord Ralph calmly. 'I think we can be sure he died a noble death in battle.'

'Does he know who the bones belong to, then?' Gwyneth breathed the words into her brother's ear. 'Was it a warrior saint?'

Hereward put a hand on his sister's arm and his lips formed the word, 'Listen.'

Abbot Henry took the skull between his hands as reverently as if it was indeed the relic of a saint. He drew a long breath and his brow relaxed in a look of deep satisfaction. 'Then we may be sure—' he began.

'Wait! There's more than one body!' The speaker was Brother Peter, a monk so ancient that Gwyneth had often wondered if he had helped to build the old church, hundreds of years before. Abbot Henry shot him a look of disapproval, but Brother Peter seemed not to notice. His voice shook as he reached eagerly into the hollowed trunk with claw-like, age-spotted hands. 'See, here is another skull . . . and hair!'

A heartbeat too late, Brother Padraig grabbed the ancient monk's wrist, then let out a grunt of annoyance.

Brother Peter slowly withdrew his hands, gazing at them in wonderment. 'Her hair was gold, all gold . . .' he whispered. 'It crumbled to nothing when I touched it.'

Abbot Henry tightened his lips. 'A second body—a woman's?' he asked Brother Padraig.

The infirmarian bent over the coffin again, examining the contents without touching them. Then he nodded. 'I think so. There are two sets of bones here, and the second set is of much greater delicacy, as you can see, Father.'

19

Gwyneth exchanged a glance with her brother, seeing her surprise mirrored in his hazel eyes. Why would a saint be buried with a woman? Or perhaps there were two saints? Abbot Henry was looking even more pleased by this discovery, as if the heavens had opened and the angels themselves rained down enough gold for him to finish rebuilding his abbey.

'Then my prayers have been answered, and the ancient stories are true.' There was a gleam of triumph in Abbot Henry's eyes. 'The coffin will stay here, along with the relics we saved from the fire,' he decided. 'We will decide in Chapter what we should do next.'

Gwyneth felt a pang of regret that she and Hereward would be unable to eavesdrop on the monks' daily council, when they met to discuss abbey business. She wanted to find out how Abbot Henry and Lord Ralph seemed to know more about who had been buried in the coffin than most of the monks. But she resigned herself to waiting for an explanation until the news made its way to their father's inn.

Hereward fastened his hand around her wrist, and drew her towards the chapel door.

But before they had gone more than two or three paces, Lord Ralph said, 'But my lord abbot, can we be sure?'

'Do you really have any doubts?' Abbot Henry raised his brows. 'Are you forgetting the cross we found buried above the coffin when first we began to dig?'

Gwyneth halted, shaking off Hereward's hand. What cross? She watched closely as the abbot nodded to Brother Padraig, who went over to the Lady Chapel altar and returned carrying a rough-hewn square two handspans long, smeared with dirt but with enough of a gleam to suggest that it was made of metal. When Brother Padraig offered it to the abbot, Gwyneth caught a glimpse of lettering on it, but she was too far away to make out what it said. Geoffrey Mason had taught Gwyneth her letters so that she could help him keep an inventory of provisions at the Crown, but the engraving on the cross was worn away and half-hidden under clods of earth, nothing like her father's clear handwriting on a piece of parchment.

Abbot Henry handed the cross to Lord Ralph. 'You see the inscription, my lord,' he pointed out. '*Hic iacet sepultus inclitus rex Arturus in insula Avalonia.*'

A gasp of astonishment went up from the monks around the coffin. Gwyneth shot a look of frustration at Hereward.

Then Brother Timothy spoke, with a half glance behind him to where Gwyneth and Hereward were standing. Was it just Gwyneth's imagination, or was his voice slightly raised as if he wanted to be sure they could hear? ' "Here lies buried the famous King Arthur in the island of Avalon",' he translated carefully. 'Truly, Father, the abbey is greatly blessed.'

Gwyneth spun round to gaze in disbelief at Hereward. Could it really be true, that the coffin held the bones of King Arthur himself?

'You see, Lord Ralph,' the abbot went on, 'all the stories say that after his last battle King Arthur was brought to the Isle of Avalon. And it is common belief that Avalon is here, at Glastonbury.' He paused, and though his voice was solemn his eyes shone with triumph. 'I believe that we have found the grave of King Arthur and Queen Guinevere.'

Chapter Two

Gwyneth pushed open the door to the taproom of the Crown Inn and carefully slipped inside, balancing a heavy tray of clean mugs in both hands. A knot of villagers were clustered round the trestle table nearest the door to the yard and she edged nearer, wondering if she might pick up some gossip about the wonderful discovery at the abbey earlier that day.

'Henry of Truro!' someone exclaimed. 'Sure as I'm sitting here.'

Gwyneth recognized the voice, and moved closer so she could see the speaker. Jack Chapman the pedlar often visited the Crown with goods to sell. About a twelvemonth ago, when money was more plentiful, Gwyneth's father had bought her a painted wooden doll from Jack's pack, and a cup and ball for Hereward. The pack, a huge bundle covered in canvas and bound with leather straps, was on the floor beside the bench where the pedlar was sitting.

'Henry of Truro?' echoed Dickon Carver, the village carpenter, his mouth open in surprise. 'That villain—the king's enemy! Did you see him yourself, Jack?'

'I did not.' The pedlar took a long draught from his pewter mug of ale and let out a sigh of satisfaction. 'But I spoke to someone who did. Henry of Truro—and men with him—is living in the Welsh hills just across the border.'

'I heard tell he was in France,' Master Carver said doubtfully.

'No, he came back.' Jack's small black eyes glittered with excitement. 'You'll have heard how he tried to have Richard murdered on the way to his crowning, but the plot was discovered in time. Richard pardoned him, and sent him into Wales but if you ask me, there'll be more trouble from him yet. With King Richard away in the Holy Land, Henry will take any chance he can get to seize the throne.'

In spite of the dramatic subject matter of Jack's gossip, Gwyneth felt a little disappointed. The pedlar visited the abbey, too, and might be expected to have more news about King Arthur's bones. Gwyneth was so worried about what was happening in the village, she hardly ever thought about King Richard and his Crusade, or wondered what might befall the country while its king was away fighting in a distant land.

She missed Dickon Carver's reply; the next thing she heard was Jack Chapman thumping his ale mug on the table. 'Henry is Richard's cousin,' he pointed out. 'He wants to be king, my friend, and nothing will stop him.' He banged the mug again and Hankin, one of the potboys, came scurrying up with a jug to refill it.

Jack took another long drink and wiped his beard on his sleeve. 'If you ask me,' he went on, 'Henry is looking for support. Men and money. Then when he's ready . . .'

Gwyneth watched breathlessly as he drew one hand across his throat. She hovered for a moment longer, hoping to hear more news, but at that moment her father appeared from the door to the cellar, wiping his hands on his apron as he hurried over to the pedlar's table with a broad smile on his face.

'Welcome, Jack,' he said. 'Will you be wanting a meal? Idony has some good fat geese roasting.'

Jack Chapman rubbed his hands. 'I will that, Master Mason. Mind you,' he added, 'I've just come from Wells, and you wouldn't believe the food I had from the dean's table.'

'The dean's table?' One of the villagers laughed derisively. 'Get along with you, Jack— you never ate with no dean!'

'Well, maybe not.' The pedlar winked. 'But if you know the way to his kitchens . . . The priests at Wells eat like lords!'

Laughter greeted his words. Geoffrey Mason joined in, and then turned to take the tray of mugs from Gwyneth. 'Tell your mother Jack's here,' he told her, 'and he'll want a meal as soon as the geese are done. Though I doubt we'll match the kitchens at Wells,' he added with a smile.

Gwyneth hurried back into the kitchen. As she went in her mother, Idony Mason, was spreading a clean linen cloth over a wooden tub of dough, and setting it to rise close to the warmth of the oven. Seeing Gwyneth, she snatched up an iron cooking pot from in front of the kitchen fire, where two geese were crackling on the spit.

'Just look at that!' Idony Mason exclaimed as soon as Gwyneth appeared, thrusting an iron cooking pot under her daughter's nose. 'There's a hole in there I could put my fist through!' She clicked her tongue in vexation. 'Gwyneth, take it down to Tom Smith, will you, and ask him to mend it. And mind you come straight back, now! The dough will be ready for kneading.'

Gwyneth hoped the errand would not take long. If more news of the bones of King Arthur came to the inn, she didn't want to miss it. Since mid-day she had been unable to think of anything else. Her mother had scolded her for dreaming over her household tasks, but Gwyneth couldn't explain what was distracting her without confessing that she and Hereward had been eavesdropping in the abbey.

She took the cooking pot her mother held out to her and let herself out into the inn yard. Chickens were pecking among the cobbles, and Hereward was winding up a bucket at the well.

'I'm going up to the smithy!' Gwyneth called,

27

waving the pot by its handle. 'Are you coming? Maybe Tom Smith will have news from the abbey.'

Hereward stopped turning the windlass and reached out to retrieve the bucket. 'I'll just take this to the stable for Jack's mule,' he said. 'Wait for me.'

Mindful that her mother might be watching from the kitchen window, Gwyneth crossed the yard and waited for her brother underneath the archway that led to the street. When Hereward joined her, wiping his wet hands on his stained tunic, they walked together along the road that led to Tom Smith's workshop.

'If I can't tell someone about Arthur's bones, I think I'm going to burst!' Gwyneth exclaimed.

'Well, you can't,' Hereward reminded her. 'Father would flatten us if he knew we'd been spying on the monks. You'll have to wait until Abbot Henry tells everyone.'

Gwyneth let out a snort of indignation. 'If I didn't know you better, Hereward Mason, I'd think you didn't care!'

'Of course I care.' Hereward clenched his fists at his sides. 'I know what this will mean for the abbey—and the village.' He paused and then added slowly, as if every word was an effort, 'I heard father tell mother that he might have to close the inn.'

'What?' Gwyneth stopped dead in the road and stared at her brother. 'But father would never—'

'Father might not have any choice. Use your head, Gwyneth! There's no money coming in, except from the stonemasons at the abbey. What happens if the building stops and the masons leave?'

He broke off and walked ahead, faster than before, so that Gwyneth had to run to catch him up. She loved the inn as much as her brother did. Masons had owned the Crown in Glastonbury for four generations, and Uncle Owen would have inherited it from Grandfather Mason if he hadn't chosen to become a stonemason. Instead, his younger brother, Gwyneth and Hereward's father, had taken over the business; and willingly, with a broad smile of welcome for his guests and a discreet eye for trouble that kept the rowdier customers on a short leash. Gwyneth had been born there, and she couldn't imagine living anywhere else.

'It won't come to that,' she tried to comfort her brother. 'Not now. The pilgrims will come back to see King Arthur's bones.'

Hereward gave a grunt of agreement, but his mouth was set in a thin line as if he did not quite share his sister's optimism. Gwyneth wondered if she ought to distract him with what Jack Chapman had said about Henry of Truro, but decided that this was not a good time. Knowing Hereward, he'd start fretting about what would happen if Henry plunged the country into war, because then there would be even less money to spare for rebuilding the abbey.

They followed the road along the edge of the houses towards the smith's workshop. Suddenly Gwyneth heard the sound of trotting hooves. A rider was approaching Glastonbury along the raised causeway which led across low-lying fields and marshland to the nearby city of Wells. She caught hold of Hereward's sleeve and they stopped to watch the horse as it drew nearer.

It was a magnificent black stallion with silver mountings on its bridle. At first glance Gwyneth thought its rider was a knight or a great lord, sitting tall in the saddle and surveying the village in front of him with a look of well-bred disdain. Then she noticed that his head was shaved apart from a ring of dark hair above his ears and he wore a habit under his black cloak, with the ivory beads of a rosary twisted around his girdle.

'A visitor for the abbey,' she observed in a low voice, as the horseman joined the road ahead of them and disappeared out of sight around the corner.

'Did you see his horse?' Hereward said longingly. His fingers twitched as if he longed to seize a brush and add an even deeper shine to the horse's glossy coat. 'I'd give my right arm for a horse like that.'

'It's no sort of horse for a priest,' Gwyneth pointed out piously. 'I wonder what Abbot Henry will think about it. He rides a mule.'

'Knights ride horses like that . . .' Hereward sighed. 'It would be a fine day if we ever stabled a horse like that at home! Cross fingers these bones turn out to be precious relics after all.'

As they rounded the street corner and came in sight of the smithy, Gwyneth saw a small crowd of villagers clustered outside. Tom Smith stood head and shoulders above most of them, a hammer in one massive fist as if he had just come from the forge. They were gathered round Brother Barnabas, the abbey steward, and Brother Peter, the old monk who had reached into the coffin to touch Queen Guinevere's hair.

Gwyneth quickened her pace. Brother Barnabas was important enough to have brought news from the abbot. She also saw that the priest who had passed them on the road had reined in his horse outside the smithy and was listening to the conversation with undisguised interest.

Wriggling her way forward through the crowd so that she could hear better, Gwyneth brushed against the horse's glossy flank. The horse shifted and its bridle jingled as it tossed its head. Gwyneth felt its hoof graze her foot and she leaped backwards, colliding with Hereward who was close behind her.

'Take care, child!' snapped the priest as he expertly brought his mount back under control. He glared down at Gwyneth, his eyes the cold grey of a winter sky. 'You're frightening the horse.'

Gwyneth felt colour flooding into her face. As well as she could in the crowd, she bobbed a curtsy. 'Your pardon, sir,' she said. Inwardly she was fuming. His horse had almost crushed her foot, and all the priest could do was accuse her of frightening it!

Hiding her anger, she turned away and managed at last to pay attention to Brother Barnabas.

'. . . a special service at terce tomorrow,' the monk was saying. 'Abbot Henry has an announcement to make that will be of great interest to everyone in the village.'

'What announcement?' That was Rhys Freeman, who kept a shop on the side of the village nearest the abbey. He had a look of annoyance on his broad red face. 'We can't waste time hanging about in the abbey. We have work to do.'

Gwyneth could see that Master Freeman's scorn was upsetting Brother Peter. The elderly monk crossed himself with a shaking hand as he blinked up at the shopkeeper, who took no notice of him.

'Rhys, your duty to God is never a waste of time.' Brother Barnabas's rebuke was firm, but he smiled as he settled his hands comfortably in the sleeves of his habit. 'I think you'll find the announcement worth hearing.'

Murmurs of speculation broke out among the villagers. Gwyneth exchanged a glance with Hereward, excitement welling up inside her. Abbot Henry must have decided to tell the villagers about the discovery of King Arthur's bones! Soon the news would spread and pilgrims would flock to the abbey to see them. The village's troubles would be over.

'Momentous words indeed.'

Gwyneth jumped. The high-pitched, aristocratic drawl came from the priest on the black horse. He leant over and addressed Brother Barnabas. 'What has happened? It must be important if Abbot Henry wants to share the news with all and sundry.'

The disdain in his voice suggested that he couldn't imagine anything significant happening at Glastonbury Abbey, but Brother Barnabas's good humour never wavered. 'Indeed, Brother,' he replied. 'And you're welcome to hear it with these others at terce tomorrow.'

A flash of annoyance crossed the priest's handsome face. 'Will you not answer my question directly?' snapped the stranger.

Brother Barnabas's smile grew strained. 'Sir priest,' he said, 'the street is no place to discuss important matters. Will you tell us your name, and accept the hospitality of the abbey?'

'My name is Godfrey de Massard,' said the horseman. 'I come from the cathedral at Wells with letters for your abbot.'

Gwyneth shot a glance at her brother. If the newcomer came from Wells Cathedral, she was not surprised that he rode such a splendid horse or that his habit was made of thick new wool. The priests at Wells, so everyone said, did not keep their vows of holy poverty like the monks at Glastonbury. And no wonder, either, that the visitor carried himself so proudly. At Wells they always tried to pretend they were better than Glastonbury, their gloating made easier now by the fire that had nearly destroyed the abbey altogether.

'Then you're most welcome, Brother.' Brother Barnabas bowed his head politely. 'Let me escort you to the abbey.'

'I need no escort,' replied Godfrey. 'I know the way, and your pace could not match mine.' A faint smile touched his lips. 'No doubt your abbot will tell me about this announcement.'

Twitching the reins, he sent his horse into a brisk trot and continued along the road.

Brother Barnabas visibly relaxed as he watched him go. Turning back to the villagers, he said, 'At terce tomorrow, remember. Tell everyone.' He took a few paces up the road towards the abbey, and then swung round in an unexpectedly dramatic gesture. Spreading his arms, he declared, 'God has blessed us, my friends. Better times are coming for us all. Come, Brother Peter.'

The villagers had already begun to disperse, but Brother Peter hesitated for a moment. His head was bowed and he was wringing his hands in agitation. Gwyneth was not close enough to catch the words that he muttered. As she took a step towards him, he blinked at her with watery blue eyes, then shook his head and scurried up the road after Brother Barnabas.

In the Lady Chapel, Mass had come to an end but the doors remained closed. It was the hour of terce, mid-morning for the hardworking villagers even though the sun had dawned but a couple of hours since. Standing with her family, Gwyneth couldn't help thinking how tired her parents looked. She was sure there was more grey in her mother's hair than a few months ago, and her father's friendly smile had become strained. She peered over the shoulder of stout Mistress Flax, who stood just in front of her, hoping to catch a glimpse of the coffin. The hollowed-out tree trunk lay on the trestles where the monks had put it the day before, but the lid had been replaced, hiding the bones once again. Gwyneth wished she could tell her mother and father right away what it contained so that they wouldn't have to worry any more about losing the Crown.

Forced to keep silent while they waited for Abbot Henry to speak, she gazed round at the new building. The soaring pillars, the arched windows and the walls of finely dressed stone showed how hard the builders had laboured for the glory of God. Gwyneth liked to think how her Uncle Owen had worked here, and how even she and her brother had played a tiny part, bringing food and drink to the stone-masons. Their names might not be remembered, but their work would last for hundreds of years.

A stir of interest passed through the villagers and workmen as Abbot Henry paced slowly to the head of the coffin. The other monks remained in their stalls; Gwyneth noticed with a start of surprise that Godfrey de Massard had followed the abbot and taken up a position beside him.

'What is *he* doing?' she hissed into Hereward's ear.

Her brother shook his head, as bewildered as she was. Father Godfrey had said that he had come to Glastonbury with letters from Wells, but now he was behaving as if he was much more important than a mere messenger.

'Welcome, my friends,' Abbot Henry began. 'I've called you here today to share some wonderful news. You all know how poor the abbey has become since the fire destroyed our church. The village has shared that poverty, but through the mercy of God our suffering will soon come to an end.'

The chapel was so silent, Gwyneth could hear the shuffle of a monk's sandal as he shifted position on the flagstones. She noticed that an expression of intense interest had replaced Godfrey de Massard's usual disdain, although his heavy-lidded eyes gave away little else.

'For some time we have suspected that a treasure lay buried in our churchyard,' Abbot Henry went on. 'A Welsh bard brought us word from King Henry before he died. But we did not seek out the promised riches until now, in the hour of our greatest need. This is what our merciful Lord led us to.'

Gwyneth stretched up on tiptoe to peer once more over Mistress Flax's shoulder, and saw that the abbot was holding up the leaden cross with the Latin inscription.

'We found this first,' announced the abbot. 'It bears words in Latin telling us that King Arthur is buried here, in the Isle of Avalon. Further down, below the cross, we found the coffin you see here, made from a hollow oak tree.' He motioned to Brother Timothy and Brother Padraig, who stepped forward and lifted off the lid. 'Inside the coffin,' said the abbot, 'are the bones of two people, a man and a woman. We believe that they are the bones of King Arthur and Queen Guinevere.'

He could not have been disappointed in the response. Exclamations of wonder and surprise broke out among the villagers. Gwyneth's mother and father turned to each other, their faces lighting up with new confidence.

'God be praised!' cried Margery Carver, the carpenter's wife.

'What happens now?' That was a deeper voice, and Gwyneth twisted round to see Finn Thorson, the local sheriff, his massive frame and red head towering above his neighbours.

Rhys Freeman didn't wait for Abbot Henry to reply. 'When are the pilgrims coming back, that's what I want to know. When can we expect money in our purses again?'

Godfrey de Massard kept silence in the midst of the babble. He had looked startled when the abbot made his announcement, suddenly opening his grey eyes very wide as if that was the last thing he expected to hear. Gwyneth felt a glimmer of satisfaction that the abbot had clearly not told him the news in advance.

As soon as he could make himself heard, Abbot Henry continued. 'I shall write to Bishop Jocelin and to the king's representatives at Westminster. Soon you may expect to see pilgrims on the roads again, and the abbey restored to what God would have it be. In the meantime we must make sure that no harm comes to the bones. Would any of you be willing to stand guard here during the night?'

'What?' Gwyneth heard one of the workmen muttering. 'Stay out of my bed and freeze to death, just to keep watch on a pile of old bones? We're skilled craftsmen.'

'For shame!' Gwyneth's Uncle Owen silenced his colleague. 'What are we rebuilding the abbey for, if not the pilgrims who would visit such bones?' He raised his voice. 'I'll sit an hour or two gladly, Father,' he offered.

Abbot Henry smiled and thanked Owen. Spurred on by his example, several of the other workmen also put themselves forward, and one or two of the villagers. When Brother Barnabas had taken their names, Abbot Henry beckoned the villagers forward so that they could see the bones for themselves. One by one the men and women of Glastonbury filed past the coffin.

When her turn came, Gwyneth felt an unexpected jolt of disappointment. King Arthur had been the noblest king who ever lived, and now he and his queen were no more than a jumble of yellowing bones, their skulls empty and all their pride turned to dust. A dust that people would flock to see, but dust none the less. Then she shook herself. Arthur's day was past, and this dust was more important than any other treasure the abbey possessed. It would bring the dead king no greater peace if the villagers of Glastonbury starved and the abbey church was never finished.

As Gwyneth gazed down into the coffin she realized she was standing next to Godfrey de Massard, and she stole a curious glance at his finely-cut profile. He was taking a long look at the bones, poring over them as if they were a difficult folio in a book of theology. Abbot Henry handed him the cross; Gwyneth saw that the visitor examined the artefact with a look of deep disapproval, almost as though he would have liked to find fault with it. He seemed reluctant to hand it back so that Abbot Henry could lay it in its place on the altar.

Idony and Geoffrey Mason had stopped to talk to Margery Carver, leaving Gwyneth and Hereward to follow the rest of the congregation out of the chapel. As Gwyneth stepped through the door she noticed Finn Thorson making his way towards the gate with his wife Hawisa and their twelve-year-old twins, Ivo and Amabel. The twins had their father's wild red hair, and a reputation for mischief from one end of the village to the other. Amabel waved vigorously to Gwyneth and she set off across the turf to join her friend, only to be distracted by one of the stonemasons who was talking to Brother Padraig and a few of the other villagers.

'King Arthur's bones?' the stonemason was saying loudly. 'Well, if they are, I'm the King of Tartary!'

'It's true,' Brother Padraig assured him, his brown eyes serious. 'Abbot Henry showed you the cross that we found buried above the coffin—it names the buried man as Arthur.'

The stonemason still didn't look convinced. Then Tom Smith's brother Hywel chipped in, his blue eyes round with wonder and confusion. 'They can't be Arthur's bones,' he objected. 'Arthur isn't dead, but sleeping. And when his country needs him, he'll return. Like in the song, you know, about the green hill.'

Gwyneth felt a pang of sympathy for Hywel's childish logic, but Tom Smith smiled and patted his brother on the shoulder. 'Hywel, lad, you've been listening to too many bards!' His face grew solemn. 'But these bones, and the cross that says so plainly whose they are, well, that's more than the stuff of folktales.'

'Maybe not folktales, but I think it's a most fortunate piece of luck!' Gwyneth craned her neck to see who had spoken and spotted the shopkeeper, Rhys Freeman, with a sneering smile on his broad red face. 'Just when the abbey's short of money, King Arthur's bones turn up—all nicely labelled, too.'

Brother Padraig turned to face him. 'What do you mean by that?' he asked calmly.

'That skeleton's no more King Arthur than I am,' Rhys scorned. 'Mule bones, more likely, or cows'. But why not, if it brings trade back to the village?'

Murmurs of protest came from the people around him. More than one of them told Rhys to hold his tongue and show some respect to the holy brothers, but there were others who seemed to support him, the loud-voiced stone-mason among them. Gwyneth felt an unpleasant jolt of surprise. She hadn't dreamed that the discovery at the abbey might be the cause of quarrels among the villagers. The stonemason was different, because he wasn't from Glastonbury so he couldn't be expected to feel the same loyalty towards the abbey and the all-important pilgrim trade.

'I know human bones when I see them.' Brother Padraig was still calm. 'And you've seen how huge they are—they came from a man of giant stature.'

'It's how they got there that I'd like to know,' Rhys remarked. 'How did your abbot know just where to dig?'

'Perhaps God told him.' Margery Carver pushed her way through the crowd to stand beside Rhys and Brother Padraig. 'It's as well for us that he did. What's to become of us, if no more pilgrims come to the abbey?'

'That's true.' Hereward spoke up unexpectedly. 'Our father's inn is empty half the time.' Gwyneth shot him a look of admiration. Her brother was usually wooden-mute from shyness in company, but his fears for their father's business had lent him new boldness.

'God told him?' Rhys echoed contemptuously, ignoring Hereward. 'If you think that, Mistress Carver, you're more easily led than Hywel Smith.'

Margery rounded on him furiously, but Brother Padraig put a hand on her arm. 'Peace, mistress.' To Rhys he added, 'The information about where to dig came from a Welsh bard, as Abbot Henry told you . . . though no doubt God's hand guided him.'

'Your faith does you credit, Brother.'

Gwyneth turned, already knowing whom she would see. There was no mistaking the voice of Godfrey de Massard.

'The whole country knows that Glastonbury Abbey cannot afford to finish its new church, now that no more money is coming from the king. What better way for Abbot Henry to restore its fortunes than to find these illustrious bones? No doubt he will gain much gold from the pilgrims who come to see them.'

'Maybe that's why God gave them to us,' Margery Carver protested. 'I don't see what's wrong with that.' But she muttered the last words under her breath, as if she did not quite dare to challenge the haughty priest.

Nevertheless, he heard her. 'What's wrong with that, mistress, is that your abbot mocks God and the saints when he deceives pilgrims with false relics.'

'Are you calling Abbot Henry a liar?' Gwyneth realized it was her own voice ringing into the soft autumn air. She startled herself with her courage, but she could not hide her growing fury at the stranger's cold dismissal of the discovery.

She found herself looking up into a pair of chilly grey eyes.

'Silence, girl,' ordered Father Godfrey. 'These matters are not for you to decide. What could you possibly know of them?'

'I was there when the coffin was dug up!' Gwyneth retorted, shaking off Hereward's warning grip on her arm. 'And we've all seen the bones—King Arthur's and Queen Guinevere's.'

'Indeed we have,' the priest murmured, raising his eyebrows. He flicked a speck of dirt from his cloak. 'King Arthur's *and* Queen Guinevere's. The find is doubly convenient.'

Gwyneth opened her mouth to reply, only to close it again when she realized that her mother had appeared in the crowd and was shaking her head at her daughter, her eyes darting arrows of anger. Gwyneth took a step back, feeling her face burn with humiliation under Godfrey's thin-lipped smile.

'Come, Father Godfrey,' Brother Padraig

said briskly. 'What's all this talk of deceit? If you have doubts, you're welcome to discuss them with Abbot Henry.'

Gwyneth was grimly pleased to see that Godfrey de Massard looked disconcerted by the monk's determined courtesy. 'Rest assured that I shall do so,' he said, before turning and striding away towards the guests' lodging.

'Well!' Margery exclaimed, shaking herself like a hen settling ruffled feathers. 'Who does he think he is, gainsaying Abbot Henry's word like that?'

Brother Padraig shrugged; he seemed unaffected by Godfrey's rudeness. Turning back to Tom Smith, he said, 'Believe me, these bones are Arthur's. And God will show the truth of it.'

Tom grinned cheerfully. 'If you say so, Brother.'

Brother Padraig began to reply, but Gwyneth was distracted by her mother, who came up and gave her shoulder a stern shake.

'I never heard the like!' exclaimed Idony Mason. 'Speaking like that to the holy father! And him a visitor to our village, too.' She paused and added, 'Mind you, he'd no right to say what he did. He'd sing another tune if the bones had been dug up at Wells.' Her voice grew thoughtful, and she glanced across the churchyard to where Godfrey de Massard had disappeared. 'There was ever rivalry between Glastonbury and Wells,' she said. 'If that proud priest can find a way to thwart our abbot, he'll do it.'

'I never thought Arthur's bones would cause so much trouble,' Hereward puffed. He and Gwyneth were toiling up the village street again, carrying breakfast to the workmen at the abbey. Clouds covered the sky; the early morning light was grey and cold. 'Half the village doesn't believe they're really Arthur's.'

Gwyneth stopped and stared at him. 'Of course they are! The cross proves it.'

'Maybe,' said Hereward, frowning.

'You haven't been thinking about what Father Godfrey said, have you? You don't think Abbot Henry is lying?'

'No . . . but he could be mistaken.'

'You sounded certain enough when you spoke up in front of everyone yesterday,' Gwyneth pointed out.

'I know.' Hereward sighed and thrust a hand through his mop of chestnut hair. 'But I only wanted to tell everyone about the effect that more trade would have at our inn. About the bones . . . I'm not so sure. Think about it, Gwyneth! Arthur lived so long ago. Why should his coffin be in the very precinct of our church after all these years?'

'Well, why shouldn't it?' Gwyneth said obstinately. 'King Henry sent word to the abbot by that Welsh bard, and all the stories say that Arthur came here to die, when this place was known as Avalon.'

'Stories!' Hereward let out a short laugh. 'Stories say anything. It's stories that say Arthur isn't dead at all, only sleeping.'

Sleeping under a green hill . . . Gwyneth remembered the song the children had been chanting, almost at this very spot, two days before.

She lowered her voice to a whisper. 'Perhaps he is yet.'

Hereward gave her a pitying look. 'Sleeping? Or dead and in Abbot Henry's coffin? You can't have it both ways.'

Gwyneth trudged the rest of the way up to

the abbey gate in furious silence. Clearly Hereward couldn't feel, as she did, the strangeness of this place, how legend wreathed around it like mist and it seemed as if the heroes of old tales might come striding down the street at any moment. Shrugging off her annoyance, she followed Hereward through the abbey gate and up to the half-finished church, where they looked around in vain for Uncle Owen.

'You'll find him in the Lady Chapel,' one of the other stonemasons called over to them. 'He went up there as soon as we arrived, to guard the relics. He's got the shift between lauds and prime.'

'He'll be taking a nap, like as not,' joked Matt Green.

'I'll take his breakfast to him. He'll want to eat before he starts work,' Gwyneth offered, jumping at the chance to have another look at the coffin and the bones.

She glanced at Hereward, but he had already started handing out bread to the other workmen. She grabbed a hunk of bread and cheese and a horn beaker of ale, and made her way as quickly as she could to the Lady Chapel.

When she stepped into the shadowed

interior, the chapel looked empty. The oaken coffin lay in front of the altar, its lid on the flagstones beside it.

'Are you there, Uncle Owen?' Gwyneth whispered, taking a step forward.

The heavy wooden door swung shut behind her and the shadows thickened. Gwyneth blinked, waiting for her eyes to become accustomed to the dim light. She still couldn't see any sign of her uncle, but as she walked slowly forward she made out what looked like a bundle of clothing, abandoned on the steps that led up to the altar.

Suddenly her hands started to shake and ale slopped out of the beaker she was carrying. 'Uncle!' she gasped. The food and ale fell to the floor with a crash as she broke into a run.

Owen Mason lay face down on the steps. Shards of broken pottery were scattered around him, and a thick trickle of blood crept from under his head.

Gwyneth clamped her hands over her mouth to stifle a scream. *Dear God*, she thought, *let him not be dead*.

As she stumbled to his side her skirt brushed the trestles that supported the coffin. For all her urgency, Gwyneth could not help pausing to stare down into it.

The hollowed-out tree trunk was empty. The bones of King Arthur and his queen were gone.

Chapter Three

Gwyneth crouched beside Uncle Owen and stretched out a shaking hand to touch his lips. His face was grey and he was quite motionless, but she could feel the faint stirring of his breath against her fingers. He was still alive.

'Thank you, God,' Gwyneth whispered.

She straightened up again, feeling that her legs would hardly support her, and hurried past the coffin and back to the chapel door. Thrusting it open, she staggered outside and almost collided with Brother Timothy.

'Gwyneth?' The young monk gripped her shoulders, looking down at her with his blue eyes full of concern. 'Whatever's the matter?'

'It's Uncle Owen.' Gwyneth gestured towards the open door behind her. 'In there—he's hurt.'

Releasing her, Brother Timothy vanished inside the chapel. Gwyneth steadied herself with one hand on the rough stone of the porch wall, swallowing repeatedly until she was sure that she wasn't going to be sick. An icy sweat had broken out over all her body, and she was shivering.

A moment later Brother Timothy re-appeared. 'I'll fetch Brother Padraig. Stay with your uncle and make sure no one moves him.' He strode rapidly away, his robes billowing around his bony ankles.

Gwyneth watched him go, and began to feel a little better as the first shock of finding her uncle's body ebbed away. She took a deep breath and went back into the chapel to keep watch over her uncle as Brother Timothy had asked.

She had scarcely reached Uncle Owen's side again when she heard voices and footsteps in the porch. Hoping that Brother Padraig had arrived, she turned to see Hereward and another stonemason, a local man called Matt Green, hurrying towards her.

Hereward reached her first. Even in the dim light of the chapel Gwyneth could see the colour drain from his face as he looked down at their uncle.

'Brother Timothy told us,' he said, his voice a rough whisper.

Matt Green bent down beside Owen, reaching for his shoulder, and Gwyneth stepped forward quickly. 'Brother Timothy said no one was to move him.'

The stonemason flashed her a questioning look, but he left the movement unfinished and contented himself with crouching down beside his injured colleague and gazing into his face.

'What happened?' asked Hereward.

'I don't know. I found him like this,' Gwyneth replied. 'He might have fallen . . . but I think somebody hit him. Look.' She pointed to the shattered scraps of pottery lying on the steps around her uncle's body. 'And King Arthur's bones are gone.'

'What?' Hereward swung round and stared in disbelief at the empty coffin. 'Uncle Owen was guarding the bones . . . Do you think someone attacked him in order to steal them?'

Gwyneth nodded, meeting her brother's eyes and seeing her own alarm reflected there. Quite apart from the dreadful attack on Uncle Owen, if the bones had gone, there would be no more pilgrims for the abbey, no more hope that the rebuilding would be finished quickly and the poverty in the village brought to an end.

'Who could have done it?' Hereward wondered out loud.

'We'll find him, whoever it was,' Master Green promised, standing up. 'Sheriff Thorson will see to that. And then he'll hang,' he added with satisfaction.

He broke off as the chapel door opened again. To Gwyneth's relief, Brother Padraig appeared with two younger monks carrying a litter. Swiftly the infirmarian knelt beside Uncle Owen, raising his head and investigating his wound with gentle touches of his fingertips. Gwyneth swallowed uncomfortably when she saw blood staining the monk's hands, but she could not look away.

Brother Padraig's eyes were dark and narrowed, telling her nothing of how serious her uncle's injuries were. Gwyneth felt her stomach clench as her anxiety grew deeper.

'Oh, please . . .' she whispered. 'He won't die, will he?'

At that Brother Padraig looked up, a smile crinkling the corners of his eyes. 'No, lass, he won't die. But he's had a nasty crack on the head. He'll be sore for a while yet.'

Gwyneth felt tears pricking her eyes and scolded herself silently. If Uncle Owen was going to get well, there was nothing to cry about.

'We'll move him to the infirmary,' Brother Padraig went on. 'We'll take good care of him there.'

'Yes, I know,' Gwyneth said shakily. 'Thank you.'

She watched as Brother Padraig supported Uncle Owen's head and signalled to the other monks to help lift him onto the litter. Uncle Owen let out a groan, and his eyelids fluttered.

'He's waking up!' Gwyneth exclaimed.

'Not yet a while.' Brother Padraig held the injured man's head between his strong brown hands. 'Lie still,' he told him. 'You're going to be all right.'

'Do you know who did this?' Master Green asked, thrusting forward to stand over Uncle Owen. 'Did you see the man who hit you?'

Brother Padraig frowned and shook his head. 'This is no time for questions.'

Another groan from Uncle Owen interrupted him. 'Ask the monk . . .' he muttered.

Everyone stiffened. Gwyneth spun round to stare in astonishment at Hereward. Surely Uncle Owen couldn't be saying that a monk had done this terrible thing?

'What do you mean?' Matt Green demanded. 'What monk?'

But Uncle Owen had sunk back into unconsciousness, and did not reply. Frustrated, Master Green stepped back and allowed Brother Padraig's companions to lift the litter and carry Uncle Owen carefully towards the door of the chapel.

Brother Padraig paused briefly on the threshold and said, 'Don't be afraid. All will be well, I promise you.' Then he followed the brothers and their burden out.

Matt Green stared after them, frowning. 'I'll go and take word to Owen's wife,' he said, and left the chapel in his turn.

Gwyneth and Hereward remained looking at each other.

'I don't believe it,' Hereward asserted. 'A monk wouldn't harm anyone.'

Gwyneth shivered. She wanted to agree with her brother, but her safe and familiar world suddenly seemed like a dark and dangerous place. The abbey was supposed to be a place of refuge, meant for the worship of God and the care of all those who lived in and around its walls. How had it become somewhere a man could be struck down, and the relics stolen that could have saved the abbey and the village?

'Uncle Owen said "ask the monk",' she reminded Hereward. 'He didn't say that a monk did it.'

Hereward looked even more solemn. 'If it wasn't a monk, then it must have been somebody from the village,' he pointed out.

Gwyneth stared at him, her heart thumping as if it would burst out of her chest. 'No!' she protested. 'It can't be! There must have been a robber . . . somebody from the forest . . .'

'Use your head, Gwyneth!' Hereward sounded impatient. 'What robbers would come here? The whole country knows Glastonbury Abbey has nothing worth stealing. There hasn't been time for word to get out about Arthur's bones. Besides, a stranger inside the abbey would have been noticed.'

Gwyneth suspected her brother was right. He was always better than her at facing up to difficult truths. She herself would have

60

preferred the world always to be sunlit, but she couldn't go on comforting herself with childish optimism.

'What should we do now?' she asked helplessly.

Hereward shook his head. 'I don't know.' His voice grew sharper as he added, 'Did you see anyone near the chapel when you brought Uncle Owen his breakfast?'

'No.' Gwyneth realized what her brother meant. 'The thief must have gone by then.'

'Not for long. The monks would have been in the chapel for lauds, and the bones must have been here then or somebody would have noticed.'

Gwyneth suddenly felt cold and pulled her cloak closer. She might have missed the thief by just a few moments. Perhaps one of the brothers had lingered behind, struck down Uncle Owen and stolen the bones . . .

'I wonder if any of the monks were late for breakfast?' she said out loud.

'I don't see how we can start asking questions like that,' Hereward pointed out, practical as always.

'But Master Green and Brother Padraig both

heard what Uncle Owen said,' Gwyneth reminded him.

She turned quickly as the chapel door opened. It was Brother Timothy again, carrying a leather bucket of water and a handful of cleaning rags.

'You'd better be off home,' he told them. 'I've got to clean up here—it's almost time for the next service.'

'We'll help,' Gwyneth offered quickly, realizing it would give them the chance to search for traces left behind by the intruder. She was determined to do anything she could to help discover who had done this dreadful thing and get the bones back—for her uncle's sake, as well as for the abbey and the village.

She hurried to retrieve the horn cup and the bread she had dropped in her shock at first seeing her uncle's body, while Brother Timothy began to wipe up the spilt ale. Hereward knelt down on the altar steps and began to collect the scattered scraps of pottery. Gwyneth went to help him, trying not to look at the shards which were spattered with Uncle Owen's blood.

'This was some sort of bottle or jug,' Hereward said thoughtfully, fitting two of the shards together. He turned them over in his fingers and suddenly exclaimed, 'Look at that!'

Gwyneth peered at the piece of earthenware her brother held out to her. It had a distinctive mark on it, a star-shaped stamp cut deeply into the clay.

'It might help if we could find out who had a bottle like that,' he suggested. 'Though there could be hundreds of them.' He frowned, but Gwyneth noticed that he still stored the scrap away in his pouch.

The chapel bell began to ring for the service of prime. Gwyneth straightened up, knowing that it was time to go. For the first time she looked at the altar itself, and let out a gasp. 'Hereward, look!'

The white linen cloth that covered the altar was as smooth and snowy as before, but one thing had changed. The cross that had been found buried above the coffin, proving to the world that the bones belonged to King Arthur, had vanished.

'I've had an idea,' said Hereward.

He and Gwyneth were walking down the path

towards the abbey gateway. Behind them, the monks were filing into the chapel, summoned to prime by the steady tolling of the bell; Gwyneth wondered if Abbot Henry had been told about the theft yet.

'What?' she asked.

'You know what I said, that the thief must have been one of the abbey monks, or someone from the village? Well, I was wrong.' Hereward shot Gwyneth a bright look, as if he expected her to understand. When she looked at him blankly, he went on. 'Someone else could have been in the precinct unchallenged—someone who was staying at the abbey with even more reason to be here than the usual guests.'

Suddenly Gwyneth realized what he meant. 'Godfrey de Massard!' she exclaimed, and then looked round guiltily to see if anyone could have overheard her. 'Yes, of course,' she added more quietly. 'He was furious when Abbot Henry told us all about the bones, you could see by the look on his face.'

Hereward nodded. 'He didn't believe the bones were really King Arthur's and Queen Guinevere's. At least, he said he didn't. He comes from Wells, so he would never want

64

Glastonbury to have something precious and be more famous than the cathedral.'

A wave of relief washed over Gwyneth. She hadn't wanted to believe that any of her friends and neighbours would do such a thing—but she could believe it of the arrogant priest from Wells. Godfrey de Massard would be capable of anything, she decided, if it would bring some advantage to his own cathedral.

'If he stole the cross,' she began, 'then Abbot Henry couldn't prove the bones are King Arthur's.'

'But why would he steal the bones as well?' Hereward wondered. 'I mean, it's not as if he could take them to Wells, because everyone would know what he'd done.'

Gwyneth paused. 'I suppose he just wanted to make certain,' she said at last. 'Without the cross *or* the bones, the abbey would have nothing to bring the pilgrims back.' She felt hollow inside as she realized how the abbey and the town would become poorer and poorer now.

'It would please them at Wells to hear that,' Hereward remarked drily.

'It must have been Father Godfrey that Uncle Owen meant,' Gwyneth went on.

'Maybe. We can ask him when he wakes up.'

As they passed underneath the archway of the abbey gate, Gwyneth spotted a little knot of people in front of Rhys Freeman's shop. The shopkeeper himself was there, legs apart and thumbs tucked into his belt, which strained around his ample belly. Osbert Teller, his dwarf assistant, was standing in the shop doorway, glaring around with pale, round eyes.

Several other villagers were there too, and one or two of the abbey workmen. Gwyneth noticed Matt Green in the middle of the group, and guessed that news of the attack on her uncle was already beginning to spread.

'Owen started to wake up, and said, "Ask the monk",' Master Green was saying as Gwyneth and Hereward came up. 'If you ask me, 'twas one of the monks hit him, and those bones have never left the abbey.'

Margery Carver let out a shocked gasp. 'That's a dreadful thing to say about the holy brothers!'

'Well, Brother Padraig shut him up quick as anything,' Master Green went on. 'And let me tell you—'

'Let *me* tell *you*,' Rhys Freeman interrupted,

poking a sausage-like finger into Matt Green's chest. 'I was out first thing this morning checking my eel traps, and I saw somebody come down the path from the village and throw a bundle into the marsh. Several handspans long, it was—big enough for a mess of bones, I'd say.'

A murmur of interest rose from the group around him and Osbert Teller nodded importantly behind his back, as if his confirmation would make everyone more willing to believe Rhys's words.

'Who was it?' someone asked.

'Now that I can't say,' Master Freeman admitted. 'The sun was barely up, and the mist was heavy. But I will say this: he was wearing a dark cloak and a hood. And he moved fast, like he didn't want to be seen once his deed was done.'

Gwyneth exchanged a glance with her brother. The abbey monks wore dark cloaks and hoods—and so did Father Godfrey.

'Did you see what his bundle was?' asked Matt Green.

Rhys Freeman shook his head. 'Once he'd gone back along the path, I took a look in the water,' he said. 'There was no sign of it.'

More questions followed, but Master Freeman had nothing more to tell. Moving away from the crowd, Hereward murmured, 'We don't know that the bones and the cross were in that bundle.'

'Where else could they be?' Gwyneth interrupted. 'Master Freeman must have seen the man right after they were stolen. It's only a few minutes' walk past the fishponds to the river where Master Freeman sets his eel traps.'

Hereward thought for a moment and then nodded. 'Well, say they were. But why throw them away? The thief could sell them—maybe nowhere near here, but he'd surely find someone with a taste for rare bones and money to spare.'

'And what would a priest want with money?' Gwyneth demanded. 'I suppose even Godfrey de Massard has taken a vow of poverty, for all he rides that splendid horse. Hereward, listen, if the bundle was King Arthur's bones, then it *must* have been Father Godfrey who threw them into the marshes. He doesn't want the bones for himself. He just wants to make sure that the abbey doesn't have them.'

At the corner of the street that led up to the

Crown, she halted and grabbed her brother's sleeve. 'Hereward, I don't suppose Rhys Freeman looked very hard for that bundle. But we could. Just imagine if we found the bones and took them back to the abbey!'

For a moment Gwyneth thought that Hereward was going to object, in that infuriatingly cautious way he had. Then he began to smile, and excitement gleamed in his hazel eyes.

'Yes,' he said. 'And then the pilgrims will come back, and the Crown will be saved!'

The sun was climbing high by the time that Gwyneth and Hereward managed to slip away into the marshes. Back at the Crown they had told their mother and father about the attack on Uncle Owen, and passed on Brother Padraig's assurance that he would recover. As soon as their regular tasks were done, they took the path out of the village past the fishponds, to the section of the river where Rhys Freeman set his eel traps.

The Tor loomed dark and forbidding above their heads, the small, simply-built church of

St Michael on its summit outlined against a pale autumn sky. The lower slopes were covered in thorn bushes, but here at the foot of the hill were clumps of sedge and rushes. They headed for the river, which had carved out steep sandy banks through the marshy ground, their line marked by a row of greyish willow trees, pollarded for basket-making. The trees rustled in the breeze and trailed their leaves on the surface of the water.

Unseen birds exchanged soft, trilling calls; Gwyneth caught a glimpse of a heron stalking majestically along in the shallows and heard the plop of a water rat launching itself into the river.

The path from the village was raised above the marshy ground, but Gwyneth and Hereward had to leave it to reach the water's edge. Sometimes in summer the land here was dry enough to graze cattle, but now it was soaked by the autumn rains, and the river was running high. Water welled up around Gwyneth's feet as she picked her way towards the river bank and filled up the footprints she left behind. She felt the cold liquid begin to soak through a hole in her shoe.

'This is where Rhys Freeman sets his eel traps,' she called to Hereward, who was following a few yards behind her, poking into pools and hollows with a long branch he had picked up on the way. 'Godfrey must have thrown the bundle in somewhere round here.'

'We don't know yet it was Godfrey,' Hereward reminded her. He joined her at the river's edge, gazing down into the brown, peaty water as it swirled past. 'I can't see anything,' he said. 'The current might have carried it away by now.'

'Whoever threw the bundle in picked a good place,' Gwyneth said. 'Anywhere else, it would just have sunk.'

'Yes—and I wonder if Father Godfrey knows the river that well.'

Gwyneth parted a clump of overhanging grasses to peer into the water below. 'He might have followed Master Freeman,' she suggested. 'Eels need a good current, everybody knows that. Let's search downstream,' she added. Her gaze flicked to and fro over the surface of the water and into the hollows under the bank. 'I just hope the bones aren't damaged.'

She broke off when she heard a footfall

behind her. Spinning round, she looked up to see a man striding across the marshy ground towards her. His tall, broad-shouldered figure was a dark outline against the clear sky, and his hood was pulled down to hide his face.

Gwyneth's heart began to pound. *He's come back*, she thought as terror stabbed through her. *The man who attacked Uncle Owen and stole the bones. He's come back for them . . .*

Chapter Four

A sharp cry from Hereward startled Gwyneth and she looked round to see her brother swaying on the very edge of the river. Before Gwyneth could grab him his feet slipped on the muddy ground and he plunged into the water. He just managed to keep himself upright by clutching at a willow bough, the current rushing around his knees.

Gwyneth reached out a hand to him, but he shook his head. His face was white with pain. 'My foot's trapped in something!' he gasped.

Gwyneth's heart lurched as she felt a hand on her shoulder, and she braced herself for the stranger to throw her into the river beside her brother. Twisting in his grip to face him, determined to defend herself and Hereward, she saw him raise his other hand to push back his hood, revealing a tanned, bony face and piercing blue eyes. Relief flooded through

73

Gwyneth when she saw that he was smiling kindly.

'Please help us!' she begged.

Without speaking, the man thrust her gently back onto firmer ground and waded into the river until he was standing beside her brother. He bent down and reached under the water, searching for whatever it was that had trapped Hereward's foot. Gwyneth noticed that he was wearing a wooden cross on a thong around his neck. The rough brown garment he wore was in the style of a monk's habit, bound with a rope girdle at his waist, though it wasn't black like the Benedictine monks' habits at Glastonbury Abbey.

After a few moments the stranger gave a sharp tug and Hereward let out a yell of pain. Gwyneth watched in amazement as the stranger hauled a stout wicker basket out of the river. As it broke the surface, a long eel slithered out of a hole in the side and vanished with a splash.

'It's one of Master Freeman's eel traps!' Gwyneth exclaimed.

The stranger tossed the broken trap onto the bank and put a hand under Hereward's arm to help him out of the river. Gwyneth saw that her brother's ankle was deeply scratched where his foot had crashed through the wicker trap. Blood was oozing out and mingling with the river water.

'Hereward, can you walk?' She hurried forward and examined the wound more closely.

'I'm not sure,' said Hereward. He winced as he put his foot to the ground, and at once the stranger lifted him and carried him to a fallen tree-trunk not far away, a refuge from the marshy ground. Setting Hereward down, he loosened the strings of a leather pouch that hung at his girdle and took from it a square of cloth and a smaller package which he unrolled to reveal a bundle of dried leaves. He selected a few of them with his thin brown fingers, laid them on the cloth, then bound the poultice around Hereward's ankle.

Gwyneth saw the pain lift from her brother's face. He looked up into the stranger's eyes and breathed, 'Thank you!'

'Yes indeed, thank you, sir,' Gwyneth echoed.

The man gave her a captivating smile but he still did not speak. Splashing his way through the marsh to the nearest tree, he broke off a stout branch and held it out to Hereward to use as a crutch. Then he inclined his head in farewell, picked up the sodden skirts of his robe, and turned to make his way upstream.

Gwyneth and Hereward were left staring after him.

'I wonder who that was? He rescued you from that trap without saying a word!' Gwyneth said when the man had disappeared among the willow trees. 'Do you think he's a mute?'

'Perhaps he's a hermit,' suggested Hereward. 'They often take a vow of silence, don't they?' He flexed his injured ankle. 'It hardly hurts at all now.'

Gwyneth's gaze remained fixed on the spot where the hermit had disappeared. Well-hidden in the woodland on the slopes of the Tor were two or three cells, roughly built of stone or hollowed out of the hill itself, where hermits sometimes came to live alone in a strange life of prayer and solitude. Most of them were old, and Gwyneth privately thought that one or two of them must be a little mad—she certainly couldn't imagine being unable to talk to people. But this hermit seemed younger, more filled with energy, than the few hermits Gwyneth had met before, and she could not help wondering why he had chosen to live in silence, away from the comforting bustle of a town. And he had such skill with healing herbs, which suggested he was a very unusual hermit—it was a real mystery.

A few spots of icy rain began to fall, rousing her from her thoughts. 'We'd better get home,' she said. 'You'll need to rest your foot.'

'My foot will be all right,' Hereward insisted, getting up to prove it. 'We can go on searching for that bundle if you like.'

'No,' Gwyneth said. 'It'll take us long enough to get back as it is.'

But as they turned to go, she couldn't resist looking back once more at the river. Somewhere under that silky brown surface King Arthur's bones might be resting, rolled along by the current until they were buried in the silt of the river bed, never to be found again.

As Gwyneth and Hereward approached the Crown, they saw a cart drawn by a white mule turning under the archway into the courtyard. It was followed by a man on a chestnut horse.

'New guests!' Hereward exclaimed.

He quickened his pace, limping along with the branch to help him. His injured ankle was giving him very little trouble, though the walk had tired him. Whatever the herbs were that the hermit had used, Gwyneth reflected, they must be powerful.

They reached the courtyard in time to see the horseman jumping down from the saddle. Hereward dropped his crutch and hopped forward to take the horse's reins, his duty as an innkeeper's son overcoming any concern for his injury. 'Welcome, sir,' he said. 'Let me take care of the horse for you.'

The horseman handed over the reins and dug in the pouch hanging from his belt for a coin. He was a tall man with close-cropped, reddish hair, and he wore a plain russet tunic with a cloak of brown wool over it, and a sword at his side. He had the look of a fighting man—some lord's man-at-arms, Gwyneth guessed.

'Thanks, lad,' he said, tossing a coin at Hereward's feet. 'Where's the innkeeper?'

'That's my father, sir,' Hereward replied, stooping to retrieve the coin without letting go of the horse's reins. 'My sister will find him for you.'

The man swung round towards Gwyneth, and she saw with a shock of surprise that he had one blue eye and one brown. She dropped a curtsy. 'I'll call my father at once, sir.'

Hereward led the horse away, stroking its nose and talking softly to it as he went. It was a good horse—not so magnificent as Father Godfrey's, but better than most of those that were stabled at the Crown. Gwyneth reflected that the man's lord must be wealthy, to mount his men-at-arms so well. The man must have travelled some distance, too, for the horse looked tired and mud-spattered.

Gwyneth meant to hurry indoors and find her father, but before she reached the door of the inn she found herself face to face with the driver of the mule cart. Delicate white hands pushed back the hood of a green cloak to reveal the face of a beautiful young woman, framed in silken tresses of raven-black hair. Her eyes were a startling shade of green; emeralds set in gold glittered on her fingers and in her ears.

Gwyneth curtsied deeply. 'Good day to you, my lady.'

Soft laughter rang out above her head and a white hand reached out to lift her up. 'Not "my lady", child,' said a musical voice. 'My name is Marion le Fevre. I need a room here—a large room, if you have one.'

'Oh, yes, mistress, we have a fine room,' Gwyneth replied. 'I'm sure you'll like it. I'll call my father.'

She picked up her skirts and hurried into the inn, unwilling to have the lady—for she *must* be a lady, whatever she said—kept waiting in the rain for any longer than necessary. She found Geoffrey Mason in the taproom and he called Hankin and his brother Wat at once to carry Mistress le Fevre's luggage up to the inn's best bedchamber.

'Well met, Gwyneth,' her father said, rubbing his hands with satisfaction. 'Let's hope she stays a long time!'

Returning to the yard, Gwyneth saw that Hereward had begun to unharness the mule. The cart was piled with boxes of stout wood and flat bales wrapped in canvas—far more baggage than one woman and her escort would need. Mistress le Fevre's escort snapped out orders to Hankin and Wat as they began the unloading, while the lady herself smiled at them and spoke more gently.

'Please take care,' she begged with a winning smile. 'Some of my possessions are most precious.'

'I'll show you the room, mistress,' Gwyneth offered, and was rewarded with a warm look from those wonderful green eyes.

'Lead on, child, and thank you.'

Gwyneth led the way up the narrow stairs to the room at the back, overlooking Idony Mason's herb garden. It was the biggest bedchamber the inn had, and in the days when pilgrims came regularly Geoffrey Mason had kept it for his noblest visitors. Gwyneth hoped that Mistress le Fevre would like it; it would be dreadful if she didn't and went away to stay somewhere else.

She need not have worried. As Mistress le Fevre stepped over the threshold she spread out her hands and looked around her with delight. 'So much space!' she exclaimed. 'And such a big window! The light will be excellent.'

Gwyneth went to push the shutters open; though the day was cold, the air in the room needed freshening.

'I need a good light,' Mistress le Fevre went on, 'because I shall be working here.'

'Working?' Gwyneth asked.

'I'm an embroideress, child. I've come to Glastonbury to make altar cloths for the new abbey church, and vestments for the priests to wear in the services.'

So that's what's in all the bundles and boxes! Gwyneth thought. Embroidery frames, fabric, and threads. She felt suddenly hopeful, as if a ray of sunlight had struck through the grey clouds. The restoration of the abbey seemed a little nearer.

'You'll need to stay a long time, mistress?' she enquired.

'Yes. In fact, I think I must look for a house here in Glastonbury, but for the time being this inn will do very well.' The young woman rewarded Gwyneth with another of her dazzling smiles.

Hankin hauled the first of the boxes into the room and, following Mistress le Fevre's directions, set it down at the far end. Wat staggered after him with one of the canvas-covered bales under each arm.

'I'll help you unpack if you like, mistress,' Gwyneth offered. 'And will you be needing another room for your companion?'

'Just for a night or two, to rest his horse,' Mistress le Fevre replied. 'And then Master Hood will be leaving.'

Hankin returned with Wat, carrying the rest of the boxes, and Hereward appeared, hauling a large bundle. 'This is the last, mistress,' he announced. 'Your mule is well stabled. We'll take good care of it.'

'I'm sure you will.' Marion le Fevre bestowed a smile of gratitude on him. 'I'm fortunate to find such an excellent inn, and such wonderful people to help me. Tell me your names, my dears.'

'I'm Gwyneth, and this is my brother Hereward. Please, mistress,' Gwyneth ventured after hesitating a moment, 'will you show us the work you do?'

She was afraid that she was asking too much, and that Mistress le Fevre might think she was a nuisance. But the embroideress threw back her hair with a ripple of laughter.

'Of course, if it interests you.' She threw open the lid of the largest chest and extracted a length of heavy white silk that was partly covered by embroidery. 'See,' she said, 'this will become a cope for your abbot to wear when he celebrates Mass.' Gold and silver thread had been worked over the silk in elaborate patterns, while rainbow-coloured threads outlined lilies and roses.

'It's beautiful!' Gwyneth gasped. She could hardly remember the vestments and altar cloths from the old church, but she was sure they could not have been half as exquisite as this.

'This gold is for festivals,' Marion le Fevre went on, pulling more lengths of silk out of the chest. 'And here is green, the colour of hope and new life, and scarlet for the blood of saints and martyrs.' She gave Gwyneth a shy smile. 'It will take a long time, but the new church shall have the best work I can create.'

'When will you go to the abbey?' Gwyneth asked. 'We can show you the way if you like. It's not far from here.'

Marion le Fevre looked up, her slender fingers clutching at the scarlet silk. 'Oh no, my child!' she exclaimed. 'I will never, ever, set foot in the abbey grounds!'

Chapter Five

Gwyneth stared at the embroideress. Her face was pale and her eyes were huge, brimming with tears.

'What's the matter?' she asked anxiously.

Marion le Fevre let out a shaken sigh. 'I'm sorry,' she murmured, beginning to smooth out the silk she had crumpled. 'I didn't mean to startle you. It's just that the fire destroyed so much, and I don't think I could bear to see the burnt remains of the walls and remember how beautiful it used to be.'

'Most of the rubbish has been cleared away,' Hereward told her. 'There's not much to see except for the walls of the new church, and the Lady Chapel is almost finished.'

Mistress le Fevre shook her head sadly. 'Truly, I couldn't bear it. Even thinking about it makes me want to weep. So much was lost—so much.'

'But how will you make the altar cloths if you can't go into the chapel?' Hereward persisted.

The embroideress shot a glance at him through her lashes, and a ghost of her delightful smile returned. 'Now I've met you and your sister, I hope that you might help me.'

'Of course we will!' Gwyneth said at once. 'What do you want us to do?'

'To begin with, measure the altar,' Mistress le Fevre replied. She laid down the length of silk on the bed and took a coil of twine out of one of the smaller boxes. 'Here, take this. Make knots to show the height and width and depth of the altar, so that I know the size the altar cloths must be.'

She held out the twine to Gwyneth, who took it from her, conscious that her own hands looked grubby and sturdy beside the embroideress's delicate white fingers. 'Won't you have to go and see Abbot Henry?' she asked. 'To discuss the designs with him?'

'Abbot Henry has written to me with all his wishes,' Marion le Fevre explained. 'And later I must show the designs to Lord Ralph FitzStephen, but perhaps he will be kind enough to come and see me here. Since they

86

are for the Lady Chapel,' she went on, 'the altar cloths must give honour to the Virgin Mary. The first one I make will show the Annunciation, when the Angel Gabriel came to Mary to tell her she would be the mother of our Lord Christ.'

'That will be so beautiful!' Gwyneth sighed, imagining Gabriel, golden-winged with a lily in his hand, and Mary in her blue robe kneeling before the angel.

'I hope so,' said Mistress le Fevre, smiling.

Footsteps sounded in the passage outside and Idony Mason came into the room, carrying a tray. 'I've brought you a jug of hot cordial, mistress,' she said. 'You'll need something to warm you on a raw day like this. And some of my spice bread. There'll be a proper meal later, if you want it.'

'You're so kind to me!' Marion le Fevre clasped her hands together as Gwyneth's mother set the tray down on the table and poured a cup of cordial from an earthenware jug. A warm scent of spices drifted into the room. 'I know I'm going to be well looked after here.'

'We'll do our best,' Idony said. 'And,

mistress, your man Master Hood is waiting downstairs for you, wanting to know if you have any orders for him.'

'I'd better speak to him,' the embroideress said. 'Send him up, please.'

'Mother,' Gwyneth began, 'may we go up to the abbey? Mistress le Fevre is going to make altar cloths, and she wants us to take some measurements.'

'Not today,' her mother replied. 'There's a pile of linen waiting to be laundered, and we need firewood for the kitchen. Tomorrow you may go, and welcome.'

'Thank you, tomorrow will do very well,' said Marion le Fevre. 'Today I must unpack, and set up my embroidery frame.'

'And when you go to the abbey,' Idony Mason added to Gwyneth, 'don't forget to see Brother Padraig and ask him how your Uncle Owen is getting on.' She clicked her tongue. 'I don't know what this place is coming to!'

'Oh?' Marion le Fevre's face was instantly distressed. 'Has there been some trouble?'

Gwyneth and Hereward left their mother to tell the new guest the story of the discovery of Arthur's bones and how they had been stolen and their uncle injured, while they went to look for Master Hood and give him his mistress's message. In spite of their difficulties, Gwyneth couldn't help feeling that with the arrival of the embroideress better times were on their way after all.

By the following day the rain had settled into a steady downpour, pattering onto the cobbles of the inn yard and forming puddles in the ruts of cartwheels in the street outside. Gwyneth wrapped her cloak tightly around her and Hereward pulled up his hood as together they hurried towards the abbey gates. Hereward was hardly limping at all now; he had discarded the crutch the hermit had given him, though he still kept the bandage around his injured ankle.

On their way they passed the market-place; a few traders had set up their stalls, but in the cold and wet there were few customers to examine the goods on offer. Rhys Freeman was standing in his shop doorway, watching the stall-holders with an ill-tempered expression on his fleshy face as if he disapproved of the competition. Gwyneth and Hereward avoided his gaze and turned under the archway that led into the abbey precinct.

As they splashed along the path leading to the Lady Chapel they heard the sound of chanting coming from inside.

'The monks must still be at terce,' said Hereward. 'We'll have to wait.'

'At least we can shelter,' Gwyneth said, ducking into the porch and unwinding her cloak. She shook off the worst of the rainwater and shivered as she draped the wet wool back over her shoulders.

Standing in the chapel porch, she could hear nothing but the monks' chanting and the soft hiss of the rain. No sound of the workmen's hammers from the site of the new church; work had still not started again. Gwyneth's anxieties came crowding back like gulls on a newly-ploughed field. Without the bones and the cross, there might not even be any reason to finish the church. Marion le Fevre's beautiful altar cloths would never be admired or treasured alongside the few relics that had escaped the fire.

No! Gwyneth clenched her hand hard round the coil of twine the embroideress had given her. *We'll do something—somehow. We have to find those bones!*

At length the chanting drew to an end and the chapel doors opened to let the monks come out, drawing the hoods of their habits over their heads when they saw the heavy rain. A few of the villagers had attended the service too, and one stranger, a grey-haired man Gwyneth hoped was a loyal pilgrim. As they hurried off to their daily tasks no one noticed Gwyneth and Hereward waiting in the porch, except for Brother Timothy, who returned their smiles but did not have time to stop and speak.

Gwyneth watched for Brother Padraig and timidly touched his sleeve as he appeared, one of the last to leave.

'How is Uncle Owen?' she asked, her stomach churning as she waited for his answer.

Brother Padraig's dark eyes rested on her kindly. He folded work-roughened hands in front of him and smiled reassuringly. 'He's doing well. Sleeping, and with God's good help there will be no lasting damage.'

Gwyneth felt tears of relief stinging her eyes, and blinked them back. 'Thank you!' she said. 'We're all so grateful to you.'

'No need,' said Brother Padraig. 'I'll send word to the inn if there's any change.' He was about to go on when he noticed the bandage on Hereward's leg. 'What's the matter, lad? Have you hurt yourself?'

'It's nothing,' Hereward replied. 'I scratched my leg yesterday, but one of the hermits from the Tor put a bandage on it. It stopped hurting right away.'

Brother Padraig nodded. 'There are many such men around the Tor,' he said. 'They make good use of the plants they find in the woods. But if your scratch doesn't heal, come and see me.'

'Thank you, Brother,' said Hereward. 'May we go into the chapel and measure the altar?'

At Brother Padraig's puzzled look, Gwyneth quickly explained about Marion le Fevre's arrival and her need for the measurements so that she could begin work on the altar cloths.

'I remember Father Abbot telling us she would be coming,' Brother Padraig said. Sounding mildly curious, he added, 'I'm surprised she doesn't want to take her own measurements, and see the place where her work will be displayed.'

92

'She said she would be too upset to see how much had been damaged by the fire,' Gwyneth told him.

Brother Padraig shook his head. 'Women have strange fancies, so they say. Maybe in time she will feel able to come and see what we are building here to the glory of God. Meanwhile—' he gestured towards the chapel door— 'take your measurements and welcome.'

Gwyneth thanked him, and she and Hereward went into the chapel. It was warmer inside, and the air was filled with the smell of incense from the Mass that had just been celebrated. Old Brother Peter was putting out the candles with a brass snuffer on a long wooden rod, muttering to himself as he shuffled slowly to and fro. When he had extinguished the last of them he sank laboriously to his knees in front of the altar, bowing his head and striking his fist on his chest in a gesture of penitence.

Gwyneth halted, not wanting to disturb the elderly monk at his prayers, but she or Hereward must have made some slight noise, for Brother Peter cast a startled look over his shoulder and struggled to his feet again.

'I'm sorry,' Gwyneth began.

Brother Peter shook his head without waiting for her to finish and hurried away as fast as he could into the vestry where the priests would robe for the service.

Gwyneth felt a bit uncomfortable that their arrival might have driven the old monk out of the chapel. But there was nothing they could do about it. The best thing would be to carry out Mistress le Fevre's task as quickly as they could, and leave.

She uncoiled the twine and gave one end to Hereward so they could stretch it across the altar and make a knot to mark the width. As she crouched down to make sure her knot was accurate, the vestry door opened again and she heard the high-pitched, aristocratic voice that was becoming unpleasantly familiar, accompanied by two heavy sets of footsteps.

'We all need to be on our guard,' Godfrey de Massard was saying. 'If Henry of Truro should come here, he will have little respect for the abbey or its brothers. A man who would rebel against his cousin and his king can have no respect for God.'

Gwyneth risked a quick glance around the side of the altar to see the priest from Wells coming out of the vestry with Brother Barnabas, the abbey steward. Hereward had ducked down beside her, and neither of the men realized they were there.

'This is ill news,' said Brother Barnabas, a frown on his broad face. 'None of us here had any idea that Henry of Truro was in this part of the country.'

'He was sent to Wales,' Father Godfrey explained, 'in disgrace, after his last attempt to seize Richard's throne. Whether he will *stay* there is another matter altogether.'

Gwyneth remembered the news that Jack Chapman had brought. In all the excitement over King Arthur's bones, and then the theft and the attack on their uncle, she had forgotten to tell Hereward what she had overheard. Now her brother's eyes were wide as he listened to what Father Godfrey was saying.

'Your discovery of Arthur's bones was ill-timed,' the priest went on. 'Though I suppose your abbot couldn't be expected to know that.'

'Hardly ill-timed for the abbey!' Gwyneth breathed into Hereward's ear, and her brother gestured to her for silence.

'Why is that?' asked the steward.

'I should have thought that was obvious.' Father Godfrey's voice was thinly disdainful. 'Henry of Truro needs men and money to seize the throne from King Richard. If these bones have any value, he might try to steal them. Many great lords would pay well for such a treasure.' He paused and then added, 'Or don't you agree?'

'You may be right, indeed.' Brother Barnabas sounded worried.

'Of course,' Father Godfrey went on smoothly, 'since the bones and the cross have disappeared, the problem may not arise. Perhaps we should all be thanking God for that.'

'Thank God for a sin?' The abbey steward's voice was shocked. 'Surely not!'

Footsteps sounded again; the two men were making their way towards the main door of the chapel. From Gwyneth's vantage point she could see their backs, Father Godfrey tall and slender, elegant even in his plain black habit, Brother Barnabas shorter and broader, the folds of his habit untidily bunched into his rope girdle.

He pulled open the chapel door so that

Father Godfrey could lead the way outside. 'Have you spoken to Father Abbot about this threat from the traitor?' he asked.

'Of course. Like you, he seems to imagine that there is no danger to the abbey. I hope that he may not be proved wrong.'

If Brother Barnabas replied, Gwyneth did not hear it as the two men left and the door swung shut behind them. She eased herself up from her cramped position, rubbing her sore knees.

Hereward straightened up too, his eyes gleaming with excitement. 'Henry of Truro?' he said. 'He's King Richard's cousin, isn't he? Do you really think he'll come here?'

'I don't know,' Gwyneth replied. 'I hope not. He's already tried once to have Richard murdered.' She passed on to Hereward the news she had overheard Jack Chapman telling in the Crown the day before. 'Maybe Father Godfrey was right!' she said uncertainly. 'It could have been Henry of Truro's men who stole the bones.' If that was true, there was no need to go on suspecting any of their friends in the village.

To her disappointment she saw that Hereward was shaking his head. 'There hasn't been time since the bones were discovered for men to have come all the way from Wales,' he pointed out.

Gwyneth reluctantly had to agree with him. 'In that case, it must have been Father Godfrey who stole the bones,' she decided.

'You may be right. But I don't see how we'll ever find out,' said Hereward, doubtfully.

'We might. We can keep trying, anyway.'

Hereward held up his end of the twine. 'Come on. Let's get this job finished. We may as well carry on as if the new cloths will be needed, even if there aren't any bones for the pilgrims to see.' His hazel eyes glinted with determination as he knelt down beside the altar once more.

He and Gwyneth took the other measurements and Gwyneth coiled up the twine carefully to return to Marion le Fevre. On their way out, she spotted Brother Timothy hurrying round the corner of the chapel towards the site of the new church. Gwyneth realized there might be a chance to talk to him after all.

'Come on!' she exclaimed to Hereward. Picking up her skirt and cloak, her hair flying, she ran after the young monk.

As she approached, Brother Timothy glanced back and waited for her, smiling. 'I can see you'll give me no peace today, Gwyneth Mason.'

Gwyneth halted, panting, and blurted out her question without thinking. 'Was Father Godfrey at breakfast yesterday?'

Brother Timothy's smile faded and he paused before answering. As Hereward caught up, Gwyneth began to realize how tactless she had been. Brother Timothy was bound to wonder why she wanted to know. But it was too late now to take it back.

'Father Godfrey is a holy man,' said Brother Timothy. He sounded as friendly as ever, but the firmness in his voice was a rebuke in itself. 'Dean Alexander has made him assistant to the Treasurer of Wells Cathedral.'

That's no reason for us to trust him! Gwyneth flashed a look at Hereward and saw that her brother understood. If the haughty priest held an important post at Wells, he was even less likely to be a friend to Glastonbury Abbey.

'After lauds Father Godfrey went to pray in his cell,' Brother Timothy went on.

No. He said *he went to pray in his cell,* Gwyneth

thought, though she did not dare voice her suspicions aloud. Somehow she couldn't see Godfrey de Massard, nor any priest from Wells, missing a meal to say extra prayers. Much more likely to her mind was that he had been in the Lady Chapel, striking down her Uncle Owen so that he could steal the bones and the cross.

'Is Father Godfrey staying here long?' Hereward asked. 'I thought he came here with letters for the abbot.'

Gwyneth could see that Brother Timothy was debating whether to answer, a troubled look on his bony face. At last he said, 'Yes, letters from Dean Alexander.' He hesitated again, and when he went on it was as though the words were being wrenched out of him against his will. 'Dean Alexander would like to make Glastonbury part of the bishopric of Bath and Wells.'

'What?' Gwyneth exchanged an astounded look with her brother. 'He can't do that!' She knew that the villagers would be little affected in their daily dealings with the abbey, but it would be bad news for the monks who would be answerable to the Dean of Wells rather than their own abbot.

'He couldn't when the abbey was rich,' Brother Timothy replied sadly. 'The idea of another holy authority taking all of our wealth would have been absurd. But since the fire . . . since the supply of money from the king dried up . . .' He shook his head. 'It's not your worry. Pray for us, both of you.'

He gave Gwyneth a quick pat on the shoulder, and went on.

Gwyneth and Hereward walked slowly down the path towards the abbey gateway.

'That settles it!' Gwyneth exclaimed, gripping the coil of twine so tightly that the knots dug into her palms. Anger was flaring up inside her, as fierce as the fire that had consumed the old abbey. 'It *must* have been Godfrey de Massard who stole the bones. He did it to keep the abbey poor, so Dean Alexander would have even more reason to take over.'

'He must be here to spy for Dean Alexander,' Hereward agreed. 'No letters could take so long to deliver.'

'And Brother Timothy called him a holy man!' Gwyneth was disgusted. 'Somehow we've got to find some proof, and show everyone what he really is.' She quickened her pace as she passed under the archway, as if by hurrying she could overtake the truth and prove Father Godfrey's guilt.

Since they had gone into the chapel the rain had stopped. A stiff breeze was tearing the clouds into rags, revealing a pale blue sky. Watery sunlight gleamed on the wet road and more stalls had appeared in the market-place. The villagers were crowding round to look at the goods on offer—piles of turnips and leeks, smoked fish, and bales of wool and linen dyed in soft colours from plants gathered in the surrounding countryside. Above the buzz of talk and laughter, Gwyneth heard a less familiar sound—a thin thread of pipe music, rising and falling in a strange, compelling rhythm.

'What's that?'

'Let's find out!' Hereward caught her sleeve and pulled her into the crowd, towards the music. Wriggling in his wake through a knot of villagers, Gwyneth's gaze fell on a handsome, copper-skinned man she had never seen before. He wore a flowing white robe, with a head-dress bound around his forehead with a twist of black fabric. His shoulders were broad as a blacksmith's, but it was impossible to tell how tall he was because he was sitting cross-legged on a rush mat, bent over a wooden pipe, his long fingers dancing over the holes to produce that piercing sound.

In front of him was a woven basket, the size of a flagon of wine. Gwyneth glimpsed movement inside; a second later she let out a startled gasp as the gleaming head and endless muscular body of a snake reared out of the depths.

Chapter Six

Gwyneth stared huge-eyed, captivated and repelled at the same time. Used to the slender grass snakes and the occasional adder in the fields around Glastonbury, she had never seen anything like this creature before. Its glossy black body spread into a wide hood just behind its tiny, glittering eyes and its forked tongue darted in and out as it rose from the basket, swaying in time to the music from the pipe.

Beside her, Hereward looked equally astonished, while the villagers shifted around them, muttering uneasily to each other.

The snake looked for all the world as if it was under a spell, Gwyneth thought. Someone clearly shared the same idea, for she heard the mutter of 'Sorcery!' close behind her, and felt someone shoving their way out of the crowd.

The musician, who had not lifted his eyes from the creature, finished the tune with one last swirl of notes and the snake sank back out of sight. The man lowered the pipe and replaced the lid on the basket, then rose in one fluid movement to bow to his audience. There was a spatter of applause, but if he had hoped for payment he was disappointed, for no one tossed coins to him as they would to the wandering bards or tumblers who sometimes came to the town.

But the musician did not seem worried by the crowd's reaction. Straightening up, he indicated with a flourish a large covered wagon drawn up at one side of the ordinary market stalls.

'You have seen a little of the mystery of the East,' he announced. His voice was deep and honeyed, the strange accent only adding to its appeal. Gwyneth edged forward to where she could see the wagon better. 'I have spices, silks, perfumes,' the stranger went on. 'Come, see. If you like, I will make you a good price.'

Instead of a stall, he had let down the backboard of his cart and covered it with a piece of saffron-coloured silk. On this he laid out copper bowls heaped with spices the colour of flames, skeins of embroidery threads, coils of gold and silver wire, intricately carved wooden boxes. When the merchant pulled back the flap of the covering to stow away the basket containing the snake, Gwyneth glimpsed stacked bolts of silk, and caught a whiff of a heady, spicy perfume.

Some of the villagers began to cluster around the cart, but Gwyneth suspected they were more curious to see the unusual merchandise than actually intending to buy anything. There was little spare wealth in Glastonbury to spend on goods such as these, which must surely be expensive. The merchant must not know how poor the village was, or he would never have bothered to come.

Then she heard familiar musical laughter, and noticed that Marion le Fevre had appeared at the other side of the cart's backboard. The embroideress was examining a coil of gold wire that the merchant was holding out to her. Taking it from him, she ran it through her fingers and nodded in approval. 'Wasim, you always have the best.'

Gwyneth's curiosity was pricked. 'They must have met before,' she murmured to Hereward.

Her brother nodded. 'I wonder where?'

Edging up to Marion's side, Gwyneth bobbed a little curtsy. 'Good day, Mistress le Fevre,' she said. 'We've taken the measurements for you.'

'Gwyneth!' The embroideress's eyes lit up. 'And . . . Edward? No, Hereward, of course. Come and meet my friend Wasim Kharab. Wasim, this is Gwyneth Mason and her brother Hereward. Their father owns the excellent inn where I'm staying.'

Gwyneth bobbed another curtsy, feeling a little daunted by the scrutiny of the merchant's dark eyes. Hereward seemed bolder, bowing and saying clearly, 'Good day, Master Kharab.'

The merchant gave them a friendly smile, his teeth white against his coppery skin, and bowed low.

'I am delighted to meet you, my young friends,' he said, and Gwyneth found herself smiling back.

'But what have we here?' the merchant demanded.

One long-fingered hand shot out towards Hereward, who jumped. Wasim fluttered his fingers behind Hereward's ear and unfolded his palm to reveal a large square of some sticky sweetmeat, smothered in a white sugary coating. He presented it to Hereward, who took it nervously and nibbled at one corner. A huge grin spread over his face. 'It's good!'

'Of course,' said the merchant. 'It comes from the stores of Wasim Kharab. And some of it has flown over to your sister, too.'

His fingers flicked into a fold of Gwyneth's cloak and reappeared holding another square of the sweetmeat which he held out to her.

'Thank you,' she said. Taking a bite, she let the delicious sweetness melt on her tongue, and watched as Marion le Fevre examined the rest of Wasim's merchandise. The embroideress chose some of the silver wire as well as the gold, and several skeins of coloured embroidery silks.

'You've met Master Kharab before, mistress?' Gwyneth asked as Wasim dug into a basket to find extra colours.

'Oh yes, many times,' Marion le Fevre replied. 'Everyone knows Wasim. He travels all over England, and his merchandise is much the best.'

'I travel everywhere and I see everything,' the merchant agreed, overhearing them. 'I know more about this country than the king himself! And not just this country, but Wales . . .'

A cry of alarm from Mistress le Fevre interrupted him. She was looking down at her feet, where a skein of silk had fallen. Hereward stooped down and rescued it before the mud had time to soak into it.

'Thank you!' said Marion as he handed it to her. 'I'm so clumsy, and I'd hate to spoil the silk. It will make such beautiful things for the abbey.'

'Indeed, mistress.' Wasim gave her a little nod. He turned to Gwyneth, dusting gold powder from his fingertips. 'If your father keeps an inn, your mother will need spices, no doubt. Will you tell her what Wasim has to offer? I will make her the best price.'

'Yes, I'll tell her.' Idony Mason probably would like to inspect the merchant's stock, Gwyneth thought. She enjoyed cooking, and having a fine lady like Mistress le Fevre to stay would give her the chance to show off her skills.

Remembering their original errand, Gwyneth pulled out the piece of twine with the altar measurements and gave it to Mistress le Fevre who thanked her and turned to go with a word of farewell to Wasim Kharab. Gwyneth watched her making her way towards the Crown, admiring the embroideress's shining dark hair and the graceful way she held her skirt clear of the mud.

Suddenly she felt Hereward tug her sleeve and heard him say excitedly, 'See—over there!'

To Gwyneth's surprise, when she looked where Hereward was pointing, she saw the mysterious hermit from the Tor. He was half-hidden on the other side of the market-place, watching Marion le Fevre as she wound her way through the crowd. His expression was unreadable, but his gaze was so intense he seemed to be drawing the embroideress towards him with his eyes. Mistress le Fevre did not appear to have noticed him, and Gwyneth half-expected the hermit to step forward and greet her—it looked as though he knew her, for sure—but as the dark-haired young woman passed within an arm's length of him, he drew his hood over his head and vanished into the throng.

'He's gone!' Hereward sounded disappointed. 'I'm going after him. I want to tell him my ankle's better.'

He began wriggling his way out of the crowd of people who had gathered around Wasim's cart. The villagers were getting over their initial wariness, and there were far more pressing up to see what was going on.

Gwyneth found herself pushed back and for a moment she lost sight of Hereward. Then she heard him cry out, and the voice of Godfrey de Massard exclaimed, 'Clumsy child! Now look what you've done!'

Squeezing between Mistress Flax and a man in a labourer's brown tunic, Gwyneth came upon her brother, red-faced and staring up at a furious Father Godfrey. A shattered earthenware jug lay on the ground between them, while dark red wine ran into the gaps between the cobbles.

'I—I'm sorry, sir,' Hereward stammered.

'No matter,' Father Godfrey said brusquely, shaking the skirts of his habit where wine was soaking in. 'Just be more careful next time. And pick up the pieces before someone treads on them and cuts their foot.' He turned and stalked off in the direction of the abbey.

Hereward crouched down and began reaching for the scraps of earthenware, collecting them in the lap of his tunic. Gwyneth bent down and helped him. 'It would have to be him!' she said.

'I know!' Hereward groaned. 'And I honestly couldn't help it. Somebody shoved me and I banged right into him. I've missed catching the hermit, too.'

'I'm sure we'll see him again,' Gwyneth said comfortingly. 'Here, give me some of those scraps and we'll take them home with us.'

She gathered the rest of the broken pieces into a fold of her cloak, and the two of them set out along the street back to the Crown. Master Hood, Marion le Fevre's escort, was sitting on the mounting block in the inn yard, humming tunelessly through his teeth as he sharpened a dagger. He gave Gwyneth and Hereward a curt nod as they passed him, but did not speak.

Gwyneth and Hereward threw the scraps of earthenware onto the rubbish tip outside the back door of the inn. As they fell, something caught Gwyneth's eye.

'Look!' She swooped on one particular shard, rescuing it from a mess of eggshells and other kitchen waste. 'Hereward, look at this.'

She held out the piece of earthenware.

Stamped deeply into its surface was a familiar star-shaped mark. Hereward stared at it wordlessly, then scrabbled in his pouch until he retrieved the scrap of pottery he had picked up in the Lady Chapel after the attack on Uncle Owen.

Still silent, he laid the piece beside his sister's. The two marks were identical.

Chapter Seven

'That proves it!' exclaimed Gwyneth. 'It *must* have been Father Godfrey who attacked Uncle Owen.' She closed her hand over the two scraps of pottery. 'I'm going to tell Sheriff Thorson.'

'No—wait.' Hereward grabbed at her cloak. 'It doesn't prove anything. Father Godfrey *might* have brought both jugs with him from Wells— but he might have bought this one in the market, or taken it from the abbey kitchens. At any rate,' he added, 'he would *say* that's where he got it. No one would suspect him of lying.'

'Except us,' said Gwyneth.

As her excitement ebbed away she realized that her brother was right. Father Godfrey would easily be able to explain away the evidence. If they accused him without real proof, they would only get into trouble.

But I will *prove it*, she said to herself as she took the broken pottery up to her room and thrust the pieces deep into her clothes chest. *I'll show everyone what kind of a man Father Godfrey is.*

Gwyneth was woken next morning by a rattling sound at the window. Rubbing sleep out of her eyes, she pushed open the shutters and looked down into the yard. Ivo and Amabel Thorson were standing under her window.

Ivo was just about to toss up another handful of pebbles. 'Good morning, Slug-a-bed!' he called, a grin on his freckled face. 'We thought you'd never wake.'

'We're going to pick hazelnuts.' Amabel waved a willow basket. 'Do you want to come?'

Gwyneth had intended to spend the day looking for more information about the theft of the bones and the cross, although neither she nor Hereward had been able to decide how best to go about it. But it was very tempting to forget all about the problems of the abbey for a little while, and go to pick nuts with her friends.

'We'll come,' she replied. 'Wait for us, while we ask mother.'

She shook Hereward, who muttered something and tried to burrow more deeply into his cocoon of blankets. Gwyneth ruthlessly tugged them off, leaving him blinking up at her through tousled hair. But he roused quickly enough when she explained that Ivo and Amabel were waiting, pulling on his tunic and combing his hair back with his fingers.

'Look at this!' he exclaimed.

Gwyneth was retrieving a shoe from the corner of the room where she had tossed it the night before. When she turned round she saw that Hereward's bandage had come unfastened during the night. He stuck out his foot towards her and she saw that the deep scratch on his ankle had completely disappeared. There wasn't even a scar to show where it had been.

For a moment Gwyneth couldn't believe what she was seeing. 'It's like a miracle!'

'The hermit must be a very holy man,' Hereward agreed sombrely.

'We ought to do something to thank him,' Gwyneth went on as she pulled on her shoes. 'Maybe mother would let us take him some food. The best hazel bushes are at the bottom of the Tor, not far from where we saw him yesterday. He might be there again.'

She led the way down the creaking wooden

stairs, signing to Hereward for quiet, for it was so early that the inn's guests would still be sleeping.

In the kitchen Idony Mason was pulling the first batch of loaves out of the bread oven by the light of an earthenware lamp. Gwyneth took a deep breath, drawing in the fragrance of the warm bread. The smell of it made her feel ravenously hungry, though she doubted Ivo and Amabel would be patient enough to let her stop to break fast before they set off.

'Hazelnuts?' Idony Mason said when Gwyneth had explained. 'Yes, we could do with some. Here, let me find you a bag.'

She vanished into her storeroom to reappear a moment later with a small sack. 'You'd better take a loaf to eat on the way,' she added, to Gwyneth's delight.

'And may we have one for the hermit?' Hereward prompted. 'Look what he did for my leg.'

Idony's eyes widened in astonishment as she inspected the ankle. 'I've never seen the like,' she said. 'His herbs must be very powerful! Yes, take him a loaf—it's little enough for his kindness.'

Gwyneth took a loaf for herself and Hereward, and stowed a second one away in the sack. She and Hereward bade their mother goodbye and went out to find their friends. Ivo was sitting on the edge of the well, dropping pebbles down into the water, while Amabel paced up and down impatiently swinging her basket.

'I thought you were never coming!' she said. 'Oh, Gwyneth, is that your mother's bread?'

Gwyneth divided the loaf into four, and handed pieces to her brother and her friends. Munching happily, they walked out into the street. Gwyneth was grateful for the warmth of the bread, for it was a raw, cold morning and the heavy clouds overhead promised more rain to come.

They had not gone far when Gwyneth heard the sound of hooves behind her. Glancing back, she saw Master Hood manoeuvring Marion le Fevre's mule cart under the archway, with his own horse tethered behind. Gwyneth and the others drew into the side of the road to let him pass, and Hereward called out, 'Farewell, Master Hood! A good journey to you!'

Master Hood acknowledged his good wishes with a brief wave, but did not speak. He was a surly fellow, thought Gwyneth, surprised that Mistress le Fevre wanted him around her. Surely she could have found herself a pleasanter servant? Still, Master Hood was probably a strong and competent fighting man, capable of protecting his mistress from all the hazards of the road.

As they walked along, Hereward told Ivo and Amabel about his adventure with Master Freeman's eel trap, and how the silent hermit had healed his ankle.

'I'd like to meet this hermit,' said Ivo.

'Maybe you will,' Gwyneth replied. 'The hazel bushes are near where we saw him.'

'And maybe he can heal the place where Ivo hit his head when he fell out of Tom Smith's apple tree!' Amabel said mockingly. 'I fear his wits have yet to recover!'

Ivo made as if to throw his crust at her and she dodged away, laughing.

Though the sun must have been well risen behind the clouds by the time they reached the hazel bushes, the day was not much brighter. The ground seemed even wetter than before, after the heavy rain. Everywhere was the sound of trickling water. Little hurrying streams crossed the path, and pools rippled as the breeze shook droplets from overhanging boughs.

Nuts clustered thickly even on the lowest branches, always the first to be stripped by the villagers. Ivo and Amabel fell on them eagerly, pulling off the clumps and piling them in their mother's basket. Gwyneth placed the hermit's loaf on a nearby tree trunk—the very one, she realized, where the hermit had set Hereward down while he bandaged his ankle—and shook out the crumbs from her sack so that she could start to pick.

She worked busily for some time, until she heard Hereward cry out, 'There he is!'

Turning, Gwyneth looked where he was pointing. Not far away she caught a glimpse of the tall figure of the hermit striding purposefully across the marshy ground as if he was confident of finding a safe passage. She called out, but he carried on without looking back.

'Hereward, run,' Gwyneth urged. 'Tell him we have a gift for him.'

Hereward took off like a hare, dodging around the bushes. Though he called out again, the hermit still did not hear him.

'What's the matter?' Amabel's voice sounded

just behind Gwyneth. 'Where's Hereward going?'

'He's after the hermit we told you about,' Gwyneth explained.

'Hermit?' said Ivo, leaving the bush where he was picking and staring after Hereward. 'I can't see any hermit.'

When Gwyneth turned round again she couldn't see the hermit either. 'He's gone,' she said, disappointed.

'If he was ever there.' Ivo let out a chuckle. 'I think you're seeing things. Or maybe he's a ghost, and he just vanishes into thin air.' He waggled his fingers comically. 'Hey, Hereward,' he added as the younger boy came plodding back through the trees. 'I think your hermit is a ghost.'

'He is not!' Hereward retorted. 'He's a holy man, and he healed my ankle.'

'Maybe you dreamed it all—the scratch as well,' Ivo teased. 'Here, see if this will wake you up!' He grabbed a hazelnut from the basket and hurled it at Hereward, who ducked so that it sailed over his head.

Hereward's eyes lit up. 'Have at you, Ivo!' he yelled, snatching a handful of nuts from the nearest bush and hurling them at his friend.

Gwyneth and Amabel joined in, and soon the air was thick with flying hazelnuts. Her hair flying, Gwyneth pelted her friends, determined to drive them back and claim a victory.

But just as she was stretching up to a higher branch for more nuts, she heard a loud cry from the bushes closest to the riverbank. It was followed by the sound of footsteps squelching over the boggy ground, and Osbert Teller, Rhys Freeman's assistant, appeared from behind a bramble thicket. He was rubbing his bristly head, and his face was black with anger.

'Cursed childer,' he shouted. 'What do you mean by throwing nuts at me?'

'We're sorry, Master Teller.' Gwyneth curtsied and pushed back her hair, suddenly aware of how dishevelled she must look. 'We weren't throwing them at you.'

Osbert Teller let out a bad-tempered snort. A gleam appeared in his small, piggy eyes as he spotted Amabel's full basket, which she had set down by the tree trunk.

'To save bothering the sheriff with tales of your mischief, I'll take this. Master Freeman and I enjoy a handful of nuts with a cup of mulled ale when the work's done.' He snatched up the basket, ignoring Amabel's protest and giving her a hard push as she tried to catch hold of it. Though he was a handspan shorter than her, his stocky arms were strong. Amabel stumbled backwards, only saved from falling by Ivo, who steadied her by her shoulder.

'That'll learn you not to hurt your betters,' the dwarf sneered. 'And I'll have this, too.' He snatched up the loaf which had been meant as a present for the hermit and took off at a run through the trees, his stubby legs carrying him surprisingly swiftly over the sodden ground.

'Hey!' Ivo yelled. 'That's ours! Come back!'

He began sprinting after Master Teller with Hereward just behind him, but almost at once he stumbled in a patch of mud and fell flat on his face. Hereward stopped to help him up, and by the time Ivo was on his feet again the dwarf was gone.

Ivo trudged back to Gwyneth and Amabel, dripping and spattered with mud. His face was white with fury, making the freckles stand out on his cheeks. 'I'll get him,' he spat. 'I'll put bees in his bed! I'll . . .'

'Oh, don't be stupid!' Amabel exclaimed. 'That was mother's best basket! I didn't even ask if we could borrow it!'

'We'll get it back,' Gwyneth promised, tucking her sack under one arm and patting her friend's shoulder. 'We'll go to Master Freeman's shop and ask him.'

'He won't give it to us.' Ivo pulled up a clump of grass to wipe his face and hands. 'He doesn't like us.'

'Get your mother to ask him, then,' suggested Hereward.

'No, we *can't*,' Amabel said despairingly. 'It's only last week there was all that trouble about the donkey in Mistress Carver's turnip patch.'

Gwyneth opened her mouth to ask what the trouble had been with the donkey and the turnips, then decided that it would probably take too long to explain. It was a rare week that went by without the twins getting into trouble with one elaborate scheme or another.

'We'll just have to do it ourselves, then,' she said, reflecting that getting back the basket couldn't be more difficult than finding out the truth about the stolen bones. 'Come on.'

Rain began to fall again as they made their

way back to the village, dampening their spirits still more. When they turned the corner of the street that led to Rhys Freeman's shop, Gwyneth saw the shopkeeper standing in the doorway, his thumbs stuck into his belt as he glanced up and down the street.

An unpleasant smile spread over his face when he saw Gwyneth and the others. 'I thought you might be passing this way,' he said. 'What have you got to say for yourselves, hey? Attacking my assistant! *And* somebody's gone and smashed one of my eel traps. I'll wager you know something about that.'

'We don't know anything about your eel trap, Master Freeman,' said Ivo; Gwyneth could tell that he was making a huge effort to speak politely. 'And we didn't attack Master Teller. It was an accident. May we have our basket back, please?'

'No you can't,' Rhys Freeman retorted. 'Be off with you!'

'*Please*, Master Freeman.' Amabel sounded near to tears, which Gwyneth knew was a measure of her desperation. 'You can keep the nuts, but you must let us have the basket. Mother will be so angry.'

'You should have thought of that before, shouldn't you?' Cutting off any more pleading, Master Freeman retreated into his shop and banged the door shut.

'I *loathe* that man,' Ivo ground out between his teeth.

Amabel sniffed and rubbed her sleeve over her eyes. 'We'd better go and tell mother.'

'No, we won't.' Ivo still sounded furious. 'I'll get that basket back if it's the last thing I do. Gwyneth, Hereward, will you help?'

Gwyneth glanced doubtfully at her brother. She had never liked Rhys Freeman or Osbert Teller, but she had enough to worry about already with all the trouble about the bones.

Hereward also looked wary. 'What do you want us to do?'

'We'll come back later,' Ivo said. 'When it's getting dark. We'll sneak in somehow and get the basket . . . I'll work out a proper plan by then. Well, will you help or not?' he finished impatiently.

'Of course we will,' said Gwyneth. She knew that they couldn't let their friends down. 'I just hope we don't end up in even more trouble.'

★   ★   ★

The sun had gone down by the time Gwyneth and the others crept cautiously up to Rhys Freeman's shop. This time they followed a narrow path that led along the back of the row of houses, screened by bushes. In the distance they could hear the abbey bell tolling for vespers.

So far Ivo had not told them what his plan was; privately Gwyneth suspected he hadn't got one. Her heart thudded uncomfortably at the thought of sneaking into the shop. If Rhys Freeman or Osbert Teller caught them in there, she could just imagine what her mother and father would say.

'Ivo . . .' she began.

Ivo, in the lead, was peering out between the branches of a holly tree. Flapping a hand impatiently at Gwyneth, he hissed, 'Shhh. There's something going on.'

Curious, Gwyneth edged forward until she could stand next to him. Hereward crouched beside her and peered out through another gap lower down, while Amabel knelt behind a clump of tall grasses and parted the stems cautiously so she could see.

Rhys Freeman's shop stood at the corner of

the street, and from their vantage point they could see the back and the narrow alley that ran along the side. In the gathering twilight Gwyneth made out a darker shadow at the far end of the alley, and heard the jingle of harness.

'It's a cart,' she breathed.

A bobbing lantern appeared from round the front of the shop, shedding light on the bulky figure of Rhys Freeman as he held it aloft. A much smaller figure, that of Osbert Teller, scuttled after him. They stopped about halfway along the alley; there was a creaking sound, and an even darker gap yawned in the wall.

'That's the cellar door,' Hereward muttered. 'What are they doing?'

'Taking in goods,' Ivo whispered. 'Or sending them out. But why have they left it so late?'

'They don't want anyone to see, obviously,' replied Amabel. 'They're up to something!'

Rhys Freeman and his assistant both disappeared into the cellar with the lantern, leaving the alley in darkness. Even the bell for vespers had stopped. Gwyneth held her breath. Then Master Freeman reappeared, carrying a large wooden box.

At the same time, there was movement in

the street at the far end of the alley. Something white unfolded itself on the cart, looking ghostly in the dim light. Gwyneth felt icy fingers run down her spine and, close by, she heard Hereward gulp. There was a faint sound that she recognized as the backboard of the cart being let down, and the white shape leapt down to the ground. As it straightened up, Gwyneth suddenly realized what it was, and barely choked back a cry of astonishment.

Rhys Freeman's secret visitor was the Moorish merchant, Wasim Kharab.

Hereward let out a muffled snort of amazement and saved himself from tipping backwards by grabbing a branch.

'Quiet!' hissed Ivo.

Rhys Freeman paused and glanced in their direction as if he had heard something. Gwyneth froze but the shopkeeper grunted dismissively and staggered down the alley to load the box into Wasim Kharab's cart.

Osbert Teller toiled up the steps with his arms wrapped round a bundle, passing his master in the alley who was on his way back for another load. Gwyneth watched, mystified, as the two men made several trips from cellar to cart, and Wasim stood waiting.

At last the Moorish merchant held up a hand. 'Enough, enough, my friend.'

Rhys Freeman halted in the act of walking back to the cellar. 'But I've more—much more,' he objected.

Gwyneth heard Wasim's silken laughter. 'And I have all I can sell. Would you drive down the price by offering too much at once? Don't worry, my friend. I shall return soon enough.'

Grumbling under his breath, the shopkeeper trudged back along the alley. Wasim Kharab handed him a small leather bag and clambered up on the front of the cart behind the mule. There was a rumble of wheels and the cart melted into the darkness.

Osbert Teller reappeared from the cellar with the lantern in his hand. Gwyneth heard the creaking sound again as Rhys Freeman closed the doors. Then both men vanished round the corner—going back inside the shop, Gwyneth supposed.

She and the others stood looking at each other.

'What was all that about?' asked Hereward.

'We're going to find out.' Ivo's eyes gleamed determinedly. 'Come on!'

Before anyone could argue he pushed his way through the undergrowth and stepped quietly up to the cellar doors. As she followed, Gwyneth listened carefully in case the shopkeeper or his assistant should come back, but everything was quiet. She couldn't think what Rhys Freeman could be supplying to the Moor—Glastonbury was hardly a famous source of silks and spices—but she hadn't noticed anything else in Wasim's wagon.

'Locked,' Ivo reported disgustedly, pointing to the heavy padlock.

'Leave it, Ivo,' pleaded Amabel. 'We'll never get the basket back now. And if they come and find us . . .'

'We'll leave it for now,' said Ivo, surprising Gwyneth that he agreed so easily. 'But we'll come back in the morning. I want to know what's going on, and I've got an idea how we can find out.' He grinned; Gwyneth knew from experience that mischief usually followed that look. 'Meet us here, early as you can,' he added. 'And just hope it's raining . . .'

Chapter Eight

'Well, you got the rain you wanted,' remarked Gwyneth, huddling into her cloak and poking a stray wisp of hair back under the shelter of her hood. The abbey bell had rung for lauds as they set out, but now all was silent in the damp grey dawn. Gwyneth and Hereward had splashed along the track behind the shop to meet Ivo and Amabel behind the holly tree where they had hidden the night before. The window shutters on the shop were still closed.

'It looks like Master Freeman isn't up yet,' Ivo said in a low voice.

Puzzled, Gwyneth turned to Amabel. 'What has he got into his head now?'

'I don't know.' Amabel had clearly recovered from her anxiety on the previous day; her blue eyes were sparkling with mischief under the hood of her cloak.

'We've got to get into that cellar, to start with,'

said Hereward. 'Master Freeman must be up to something underhand, or he'd do it openly, in daylight. And remember, Wasim wouldn't take all he had to sell. There'll still be something in the cellar to show us what's going on.'

Gwyneth hesitated. 'But we'll have to break in . . .'

'We're only doing our duty,' Amabel pointed out. 'Father's the sheriff—he'll expect us to root out any wrongdoing. We might get the basket back, too. Thank the saints, mother didn't notice it was missing last night.'

Gwyneth wasn't quite convinced by her friend's reasoning, but she didn't argue any more. 'What do you want us to do?' she asked.

'Bring some of that,' Ivo ordered. He pointed to a heap of stones, brushwood, and rubbish that lay beside the track.

Gwyneth stared at him, but he obviously wasn't going to explain. He looked as if he was enjoying himself, in spite of the rain that plastered his red hair to his head and made his sodden tunic cling to him. Amabel, clearly in on the secret, let out a muffled giggle. Hereward gave them a puzzled look, then grinned as if he understood what Ivo had in mind.

133

Gwyneth and Amabel picked up an armful of the wet brushwood and followed Ivo, who led them cautiously into the alley, glancing from side to side to make sure no one was watching. He carried a huge stone in both hands.

Alongside the shop, a narrow channel sunk into the cobbles was carrying the rainwater away; it raced along, muddy brown and flecked with foam. Ivo studied it for a moment, judging the distance to the door of Rhys Freeman's storage cellar.

'Just about here, I think.' He dropped the stone into the channel just downstream of the cellar door, sending rainwater sloshing over his boots.

'Good idea!' Hereward's eyes flashed with delight. He lugged a broken branch across the street and jammed it next to the stone.

'Now I see!' Gwyneth exclaimed to Amabel. 'We're going to flood the cellar!'

She and Amabel added their brushwood to the pile. By now the channel was almost completely blocked. A small amount of rainwater trickled through, but most of it eddied above the pile of rubbish, forming a pool, and then began to pour under the cellar door.

'Marvellous!' said Ivo, rubbing his hands. 'Now, somebody had better warn Rhys Freeman.' He grinned at Gwyneth. 'You can tell him. He'll never trust me or Amabel.'

Gwyneth knew Ivo was right. The twins had such a reputation for mischief that most of the villagers wouldn't have believed them if they said it was a wet day.

'Good luck!' Hereward said cheerfully. 'Don't let him scare you.'

Leaving the others to wait in the alley, Gwyneth hurried round the front of the shop and began beating on the front door. 'Master Freeman! Master Freeman! There's water getting into your cellar!'

There was no response. Gwyneth went on hammering on the door and calling out until one of the shutters was flung open and Rhys Freeman poked his head out.

'What's that racket?' he shouted. 'Can't a God-fearing man get some sleep round here?'

'Master Freeman, the rainwater is getting into your cellar,' Gwyneth explained. 'All your stock will be ruined.'

For a moment Rhys Freeman gaped at her, looking angry and worried at the same time.

'Hurry,' Gwyneth urged him. 'The rain's pouring in.'

'Rubbish!' Rhys Freeman made up his mind. 'Go away.'

'But Master Freeman—'

'Go away, girl,' the shopkeeper interrupted. 'Or I'll tell your father to take his belt to you.'

'There's no call to talk about belts.' The rumbling voice spoke just behind Gwyneth and she turned to see Tom Smith. 'What's going on here?' asked the blacksmith.

'Oh, Master Smith, the drain's blocked and there's water getting into Master Freeman's cellar,' Gwyneth explained, relieved at the prospect of finding an ally. After all, she was speaking the perfect truth about the flood. 'I've tried to tell him, but he doesn't believe me.'

She led the blacksmith round the corner; by now the rainwater was gurgling steadily through the gap at the bottom of the cellar door. Further down, Hereward and the twins were clustered around the blockage in the channel.

'We're trying to clear it, Master Smith,' said Ivo, groaning as he pretended to struggle with the stone he had placed there a short time before. 'But it might be too late.'

Hereward and Amabel nodded in agreement, wide-eyed with seriousness.

Tom strode back to the front of the shop where Rhys Freeman was still leaning out of the window.

'Take yourself off,' snapped the shopkeeper. 'You've no call to come interfering here.'

'Don't be a fool, man,' said Tom Smith. 'Your goods will be ruined. Come down and open up, and I'll help you shift them.'

Rhys Freeman's only response was to bang the shutter closed.

'His head's addled,' Tom Smith snorted. 'He won't thank us if he leaves his stock to ruin. Come on.' He waded through the pool to the cellar door and shook it. 'Locked. Well, we'll soon see about that.'

He put his massive shoulder to the door and heaved. There was a splintering sound as the door gave way and swung inwards to reveal a flight of steps leading down into darkness. Tom let out a grunt of satisfaction and went in.

The four friends exchanged excited glances and crowded down the steps after him.

Gwyneth stood at the bottom of the cellar steps, blinking in the dim light that spilled down from the open door. The ceiling of the cellar was only just above her head; Tom Smith had to stoop. Water trickled steadily down the steps, thanks to the blocked drain, and the stone-flagged floor was already flooded. There was a strong smell of damp and rats.

As her eyes became used to the light Gwyneth made out a trestle table against the opposite wall. Underneath it were two or three boxes like the ones that Rhys Freeman had loaded onto Wasim Kharab's cart the night before. While on the table . . .

'Holy relics!' The awed whisper came from Amabel, hurriedly making the sign of the cross.

Gwyneth stared in astonishment and went closer. Arranged at one end of the table were a number of small lidless boxes, less than a handspan in length, made of a dull metal like lead. Each one contained a small piece of bone. Another box was shaped like a cross, and that one held a rusty nail. Yet another had a scrap of blue linen.

Gwyneth felt very confused. These things looked like the holy relics that wealthy pilgrims used to buy from the abbey, or even like some of the treasures owned by the abbey itself. But why should so many holy things be hidden away in Rhys Freeman's cellar?

Then she heard Hereward's voice, speaking sharply. 'That can't be right. Look here.'

At the other end of the table was what Gwyneth first took to be a pile of rubbish. Then she saw that more bones were lying there in an untidy heap. Beside them was a handful of rusty nails, more of the blue fabric, and most puzzling of all, a scrap of fishing net, the cords rotten and unravelling.

'We shouldn't touch them, they're saints' bones,' said Ivo as Gwyneth reached out a hand.

'Saints' bones?' Tom Smith's voice was disgusted. 'Pigs', I'd say.' He picked up a few of the nails and let them fall again. 'Nails from the True Cross, no doubt. And a piece of the Virgin's robe and St Peter's fishing net. Rhys Freeman must think we're all fools.'

'You mean he's *making* holy relics?' Gwyneth asked in disbelief.

There was a shout of laughter from Ivo. 'The old fraud!'

'Who are you calling a fraud?' Rhys Freeman's voice, loud and aggressive, came from the top of the steps. 'What are you doing in my cellar? You're trespassing!'

Tom Smith turned to face him as the fat shopkeeper stamped down the stairs and splashed his way through the rainwater. 'Rhys, what's going on here? Were you going to sell these fakes to the villagers?'

'No!' Master Freeman's face was red with anger and guilt. 'Prove that I've sold a single one in the village!'

'He doesn't have to,' Hereward pointed out. Gwyneth glanced at him, then realized they could all guess exactly what Master Freeman did with his fake relics. 'I think you sell them to Wasim Kharab, that Moorish merchant who was at the market yesterday,' Hereward went on.

'Yes,' Gwyneth added. 'We saw you last night, loading boxes into Wasim's cart.'

'Spying on me, were you?' Rhys Freeman blustered. 'It's nothing to do with you, you nosy, interfering little—'

'That's enough, Rhys,' said Tom Smith. 'Maybe we'd better see what else is going on

140

down here. Ivo, Amabel, go and fetch your father. The sheriff needs to know about this.'

'Here, there's no need for that,' Rhys Freeman began to protest, but Ivo and Amabel ignored him and scrambled back up the cellar steps.

Rhys was about to follow them, but Tom Smith thrust him back towards the cellar wall and took up a position at the bottom of the steps, feet apart and arms folded across his massive chest, making it impossible for the shopkeeper to escape.

Gwyneth and Hereward stood awkwardly beside the trestle table. The cellar was as large as the shop above, with shadowy corners away from the light from the door. As Gwyneth's eyes grew more used to the light she could see that other boxes were stacked there.

Hereward tugged at her sleeve. 'Come on, let's look around.'

'Keep your grubby fingers off my property!' Rhys Freeman exclaimed at once.

'Take no notice of him,' said Tom Smith. 'Have a good look, both of you. Finn Thorson will want to know what's been going on here.'

Hereward made straight for the stack of

boxes, while Gwyneth groped her way along one wall, feeling for what might be hidden in the darkness and aware all the time of Rhys Freeman's eyes boring furiously into her back. At first she found nothing but dust and cobwebs; then she almost fell over a larger wooden box, pushed back into an alcove and covered by an old blanket as if the shopkeeper had made a special effort to hide it.

She pulled off the blanket and cautiously raised the lid. For a moment she stared in disbelief. Amid a jumble of yellowing bones, two skulls fixed their sightless gaze on her. Gwyneth's spine tingled. She had seen these skeletons before.

'You, girl!' Rhys Freeman shouted just behind her. 'Leave that alone!'

'Arthur's bones!' Gwyneth gasped, spinning round to face the shopkeeper.

'What!' The delighted exclamation came from Hereward; he hurried up and bent over the box, then looked up to face Gwyneth with shining eyes. 'We've found them at last!'

'What's that you say?' Tom Smith loomed up behind them. There was a look of wonder on his face as his gaze fell on the bones. 'So they were here all along,' he murmured. 'Who would have thought it?'

'Master Freeman must be the thief,' Gwyneth burst out. Indignation flooded over her. 'He attacked Uncle Owen!'

She whirled round at the sound of footsteps to see the shopkeeper fleeing up the steps, casting a frightened glance behind him as he ran.

'Stop!' Tom Smith bellowed. 'Stop, thief!'

He plunged across the cellar in pursuit, with Hereward hard behind him. Master Freeman had almost reached the top of the steps when another figure appeared in the doorway, outlined against the light.

'Dickon!' roared Tom Smith. 'Hold him! He's a thief!'

Dickon Carver grabbed the fleeing shop-keeper and the two men wrestled together in the doorway. Tom Smith joined them and grabbed Rhys from behind, pinning his arms. Rhys went on struggling for a moment longer and then gave in, staring defiantly at his captors and one or two of the other villagers who had appeared, attracted by the shouting.

'What's going on?' asked Dickon Carver.

'King Arthur's bones are here,' Tom Smith

explained. 'Mistress Flax, take word to the abbey, would you? Abbot Henry will be glad to have them back.'

Mistress Flax bustled off importantly, while Tom and Dickon propelled Rhys Freeman back into the cellar. Gwyneth caught a glimpse of Osbert Teller peering through the door, only to vanish abruptly when he caught sight of his master being held prisoner.

'Now we'll just wait for the sheriff,' said Tom Smith.

Hereward was standing at the foot of the steps, his face white with anger. 'You could have killed our uncle!' he spat.

'It was naught but a tap,' growled Rhys Freeman.

Hereward's fists were clenched and he was breathing hard as if he'd just run to the top of the Tor and back. For a moment Gwyneth thought her brother might fling himself on Master Freeman, raining blows on him.

She took a step towards him, unsure whether she wanted to stop Hereward or help him, and halted as she remembered something that had been at the back of her mind ever since she discovered the bones.

She looked into the box again. The two skulls still stared up from the jumble of yellowed bones, but there was something missing.

'What about the cross?' she said. 'It isn't here. What have you done with it?' Gwyneth glared at the shopkeeper. Her elation at the recovery of the bones was fading fast: without the cross to prove what they were, the abbey could not display them for pilgrims to wonder at.

'I never took it,' Rhys Freeman said sullenly. 'I know nothing about it.'

'Do you think we'll believe that?' Hereward's voice was filled with scorn. 'Come on, Gwyneth, let's look around. It's bound to be here somewhere.'

While Tom Smith and Dickon Carver stood guard over the shopkeeper, Gwyneth and Hereward began to search again. Gwyneth was conscious all the time of the empty eye-sockets of the skulls, watching her from their box. *Did you see what happened?* she pleaded silently. *Do you know where the cross is now?*

She found nothing more except heaps of rubbish that were probably destined to be turned into holy relics, and she turned hopefully when Hereward exclaimed, 'Look at this!'

But her brother had not found the cross. Instead he was holding an earthenware jug, the kind that held wine. It was empty, and when Hereward upended it Gwyneth saw that it bore the same star-shaped mark that was on the two broken scraps they had been keeping carefully.

'This is the kind of jug that hit Uncle Owen,' Hereward said.

Gwyneth nodded her head in understanding. 'Of course—Master Freeman must sell them.'

Hereward held out the flagon to the shop-keeper. 'Did you sell a jug of wine like this to Father Godfrey?' he demanded.

Rhys Freeman didn't meet his eyes. 'I may have done,' he admitted grudgingly.

'And it came from the same batch as the jug you used to attack Uncle Owen.' Hereward's words sounded like a statement, not a question, and the shopkeeper didn't try to deny it.

So it looked as though the priest from Wells was innocent after all, thought Gwyneth. For a moment Gwyneth felt guilty for being so convinced that he had been responsible, but then she shrugged. Godfrey de Massard might not have stolen the bones and hurt Uncle

Owen, but he was still a spy for Dean Alexander and a haughty, unfriendly man. Gwyneth felt she had no cause to like him.

A stir at the top of the steps heralded the arrival of Brother Barnabas and Brother Peter from the abbey, summoned by Mistress Flax. The steward picked his way carefully down the still-wet steps into the cellar, holding his robes to his knees, while Hereward hurried to help Brother Peter. Gwyneth noticed that he looked older and more frail than ever, as if the crime committed at the abbey had struck him to the heart.

'Where are the bones?' asked Brother Barnabas, gazing round the cellar.

'Over here, Brother.' Gwyneth beckoned him over to the alcove so that he could see what she had found.

The abbey steward crossed himself. 'God be praised,' he whispered. Then he frowned. 'But where is the cross?'

'We can't find it down here,' Hereward confessed. 'Maybe it's upstairs in the shop. Somebody should search.'

'I told you, I never took the cross,' Rhys Freeman protested. 'I never even saw it.'

Tom Smith snorted. 'And pigs might fly,' he said.

Brother Peter tugged Brother Barnabas by the sleeve. 'Maybe we should believe him,' he suggested anxiously. 'Lying is a grievous sin.'

'So is theft,' Brother Barnabas replied.

'Brothers, you'd better take the bones back to the abbey,' said Tom Smith. 'Dickon and I must stay here until the sheriff comes. Then we'll search the whole place for the cross.'

Brother Barnabas nodded. 'Abbot Henry will rejoice to have the bones back. We must hold a special Mass of thanksgiving.'

He bent down and took one end of the box, while Brother Peter took the other. Gwyneth wondered if the elderly monk would be too fragile to bear the weight, but he and Brother Barnabas lifted the box with great reverence and manoeuvred it up the stairs and out into the open. She and Hereward followed them.

At the top of the steps Brother Peter stumbled, and Hereward grabbed his end of the box before the monk could drop it.

'Shall we come with you and help?' he suggested.

'A good idea,' Brother Barnabas agreed.

When they reached the abbey, Abbot Henry was standing outside the Lady Chapel, eagerly waiting to guide the precious bones into their resting-place. The tall, elegant figure of Godfrey de Massard stood beside him. His face wore a look of cold disdain; the look he gave the box suggested to Gwyneth that he was severely disappointed by the recovery of the ancient relics.

When the box had been placed reverently in front of the altar, beside the oaken coffin which had first contained the bones, Gwyneth and Hereward told the story of how Tom Smith had broken into the flooded cellar and they had come to discover what Rhys Freeman had done.

'Making relics?' Abbot Henry exclaimed, shocked, when they came to that part of the tale.

'On a small scale,' said Brother Barnabas dismissively. 'A few scraps of rubbish, no more.'

'Oh, no,' said Gwyneth, without thinking. 'There were many more boxes, but Wasim Kharab took them.'

As soon as the words were out she was aware of Hereward's horrified stare, and realized that she had laid herself open to questions about Wasim, and how she knew about his involvement. Ivo's trick with the drain would be discovered for certain.

To her surprise, it was Father Godfrey who pounced on her admission.

'Wasim Kharab? The Moorish merchant with the snake? Interesting. Go on.'

Gwyneth let Hereward take up the story, and she was very relieved when he skirted around the whole matter of how the cellar came to be flooded. Instead he said how fortunate it was that they had happened to pass Rhys Freeman's shop so early in the morning, when the drain had only just started to flood. No more was said about Wasim.

Abbot Henry's thin features were alight with happiness as the tale drew to an end. 'Truly God guided you,' he said. 'The bones are restored to where they should be. This is a great day for our abbey.'

And for the village, Gwyneth added to herself, imagining all the pilgrims who would take the road to Glastonbury again to see the marvellous relics.

Her confidence was shattered a moment later

when Father Godfrey spoke. 'The bones are restored, but not the cross. Without it, how can you prove that these are indeed the bones of King Arthur and Queen Guinevere?'

He gave a small, wintry smile and Gwyneth dug her nails into her palms with anger. How dare this arrogant cleric seem to rejoice in Glastonbury's lack of proof for their rare find? It suited him very well that the cross could not be found, for without it, the bones would be challenged in many envious quarters. Indeed, perhaps Father Godfrey had known all along that the bones were unimportant—it was the cross that needed to disappear, leaving the bones as nothing more than ancient dust.

Was it possible that Rhys Freeman was telling the truth when he said that he had not taken the cross?

Chapter Nine

Returning from the abbey, Gwyneth and Hereward saw an even bigger crowd outside Rhys Freeman's shop. As they crossed the road towards it, Finn Thorson, the huge red-haired sheriff, emerged from the alley. Rhys Freeman was with him; Master Thorson's massive hand was on his shoulder as the sheriff marched him down the road towards his house to a chorus of jeers from the villagers. There was no sign of Osbert Teller.

Ivo and Amabel crept out of the shop once their father had gone. Amabel was clutching her mother's willow basket. When they saw Gwyneth and Hereward they waved and ran over to join them.

'Master Freeman's been arrested,' Ivo told them as soon as he came within earshot. 'Father's taking him for questioning.'

'We searched the shop,' Amabel added. 'The cross isn't there.'

'Then we'll have to go on looking for it,' Hereward said determinedly.

Gwyneth agreed, though she had no idea where to start. She wished she could have searched Father Godfrey's cell in the abbey, but she knew that was impossible. 'If only we could hear Master Freeman being questioned,' she said. 'He might have been lying when he said he doesn't know where the cross is.'

'Well, we can!' Amabel's eyes shone gleefully. 'Come on!'

Gwyneth glanced at Hereward and they nodded to each other. After the triumph of finding the bones, they had to do everything they could to recover the cross as well. Eagerly she and Hereward followed their friends past the Crown and round the corner to the sheriff's house, keeping a safe distance behind the sheriff and his prisoner.

When Finn Thorson escorted Master Freeman into his house, Ivo and Amabel led their friends down a side alley into a small yard. A herb patch grew in the middle and a large mulberry tree leaned over the house, brushing its leaves against the wooden shutters.

'Where do we go now?' asked Hereward.

Ivo pointed into the branches of the tree. 'Up there!'

A rainwater butt stood at the foot of the tree, making a useful first step into the branches, though the butt had no lid so would-be climbers had to be careful to keep their feet on the narrow rim. Not far above it, the trunk forked, and anyone standing in the fork could look through a first floor window into the house.

'That's the room where father questions his prisoners,' Amabel explained.

'You go first,' Ivo said to Hereward and Gwyneth with a flourishing bow, as if he was allowing a pair of noblemen to go into a room ahead of him.

Hereward heaved himself onto the edge of the water butt and then into the lowest branches. Gwyneth scrambled up next and balanced beside him. Through the open window, she saw a room with a sturdy wooden table and bench, a storage press and a couple of stools. The sheriff was sitting on the bench with his back to the table, and Rhys Freeman was standing in front of him.

'Tell me—' Sheriff Thorson began. He was

interrupted by a tap on the door. 'Come in!' he called.

The door opened, and Gwyneth let out a gasp.

'Godfrey de Massard,' muttered Hereward. 'We might have known it!'

'Sheriff Thorson.' The black-robed cleric inclined his head. 'May I listen to your examination?'

The sheriff looked puzzled as if he couldn't understand the reason for the priest's request, but he answered readily enough. 'Of course, Father, if you want to.'

'What does *he* want?' Ivo pulled himself up into the tree beside Gwyneth, and Amabel followed him. There was hardly room for all of them in the fork of the tree, so Ivo straddled a branch higher up, making it dip. The twigs scraped across the window shutter.

'*Shhh!*' said Amabel.

But the men inside the room had noticed nothing. Godfrey de Massard seated himself on a stool in one corner, folding his black robes around him, while the sheriff turned his attention back to Rhys Freeman.

'Now, Rhys,' he said calmly. 'I'd be within

my rights to call my men and have you whipped, but I don't think there's need. You'll tell me the truth without that, won't you?'

The fat shopkeeper nodded eagerly. His face was an unhealthy greyish colour and his eyes bulged with fear.

'How long has this trade in fake relics been going on?' Finn Thorson asked.

'I made them first for the pilgrims,' Master Freeman said in a rush. 'I didn't mean any harm. But when the pilgrims stopped coming, there was no profit in it any more. I took some to sell in Salisbury and that's where I met Wasim Kharab. He said he would buy all I could make, and come himself to collect them.'

'What do you know of Wasim?' asked Father Godfrey.

Rhys Freeman's gaze flickered across to the priest. 'No more than anybody knows,' he replied defensively. 'I didn't know what he wanted with relics, and I didn't ask.'

Godfrey de Massard gave him a long, considering look, but didn't say anything more. Gwyneth suddenly wondered if it was possible that both men knew exactly where the cross was—and why it had gone missing in the first place. After all, the bones alone would have been an armful for one man. It might make good sense if there were two thieves all along. Was Father Godfrey here to make sure that Rhys Freeman didn't give him away?

'Now let us come to the matter of King Arthur's bones,' said Finn Thorson. 'Were you intending to sell them to Wasim Kharab?'

'No!' Rhys Freeman sounded genuinely outraged. 'I never meant to sell them at all. I was taking good care of them. But there's those who would pay good money for Arthur's bones, and . . . well, I couldn't sell fakes, could I, if everybody knew the real ones were on display in the abbey?'

'Very clever, Rhys.' Finn Thorson sounded disgusted by the trader's twisted logic. 'Tell me how you stole them.'

The shopkeeper cast an agonized glance at the door, as if even now he was considering whether he could make a break for freedom. Then his shoulders sagged and he seemed to realize that his only hope lay in telling the truth.

'I knew I'd have to steal the bones before daylight,' he began, 'so I got into the abbey grounds where there's a gap in the wall for the building stone to be delivered. When I crept into the chapel, Owen Mason was there on guard. I thought he'd gone to sleep but then he stirred, and I was afeared he'd see me, so I—I hit him with the jug. I didn't mean for him to be hurt.'

Gwyneth gripped the branch until her knuckles turned white. Beside her, Hereward's mouth was tight with anger.

Finn Thorson snorted. 'So it was just a friendly gesture, was it? And then you took the bones and hid them away in your cellar?'

Rhys Freeman nodded. 'That's right, Sheriff Thorson. They've taken no harm, I swear it.'

'And the cross?' the sheriff asked. 'What about that?'

'I never touched it!' Master Freeman protested. 'I never even set eyes on it.'

'Is that the truth, Rhys?' Finn Thorson's voice was stern. 'If you know aught about the cross, best confess it now.'

'I told you, I never saw it!' Taking a step towards the table, the shopkeeper added, 'Don't be hard on me. I've lived here all my life, and never—'

'Be quiet, man,' said the sheriff. 'You'll be

locked up here until I've given your case some thought. And I'll speak with the abbot. Father Godfrey, is there anything else you want to say?'

Godfrey de Massard rose from his stool and approached Rhys Freeman. He was giving the shopkeeper the kind of look that he might have given a worm on his trencher at dinner.

'Would it be news to you, Master Freeman,' he said ominously, 'that Wasim Kharab is suspected of supporting Henry of Truro?'

Gwyneth was astonished. What could King Richard's traitorous cousin have to do with the theft of Arthur's cross? In her surprise, she slipped sideways on the branch. Grabbing handfuls of leaves, she tried to cling on and listen for Rhys Freeman's reply.

The shopkeeper looked terrified. 'H-Henry of Truro?' he stammered. 'No, I know naught of that. I'm no traitor!' Turning to the sheriff, he went on, 'You've got to believe me!'

Finn Thorson silenced him with an impatient gesture. To Father Godfrey he said, 'Is this true?'

'I do not know for sure,' the priest replied. 'But it is possible. Wasim is thought to be gathering money to fund Lord Henry's bid for the throne. Or so our news in Wells says.'

In spite of automatically mistrusting anything that Godfrey de Massard said, Gwyneth was inclined to believe him now. When she had first heard of Henry of Truro from Jack Chapman, the pedlar had said that Henry was waiting until he could gather enough men and money for another attempt to seize the crown from King Richard. And Father Godfrey had already told Brother Barnabas that he thought Henry of Truro might try to steal the holy bones to raise more funds.

'Treason . . .' Master Thorson said thoughtfully. 'It comes closer by the day, it seems. But look at him,' he added, nodding towards the trembling shopkeeper. 'If you wished to overthrow the king, would you conspire with him?'

Father Godfrey's scornful look was answer in itself.

'You're a good man, Sheriff Thorson,' the shopkeeper babbled. 'I knew you'd believe me.'

'Silence!' Finn Thorson's calm suddenly broke, and he roared at the cowering man in front of him. 'You've assaulted Owen Mason, you've stolen a priceless relic from the abbey, you've cheated the rest of the villagers, you've blasphemed against Holy Church with your fake relics. Isn't that enough, without a charge of treason?'

He got up and strode to the door, calling for a guard to take Rhys Freeman away. As he flung the door open, the leaves Gwyneth was clutching gave way and she lost her balance altogether. Hereward grabbed at her, but his fingers slipped. Gwyneth let out a shriek as she felt herself falling straight into the water butt below.

As she heaved herself out, dripping, she heard heavy footsteps approach the window above her head, and a furious bellow.

'Ivo! Amabel! What's going on out there?'

Chapter Ten

Gwyneth blew out the rushlight, leaving the room in darkness except for a sliver of moonlight creeping through a gap in the window shutters. She could hear Hereward shifting around in his bed on the other side of the room.

'What do you think now?' she whispered. 'Did Rhys Freeman steal the cross?'

'No.' Hereward's voice sounded sleepy. 'I think it was Father Godfrey.'

Gwyneth frowned into the dark. She had suspected the arrogant priest too, but now she was having second thoughts. If Rhys Freeman and Father Godfrey had been accomplices, the shopkeeper would surely have said so when Finn Thorson had been questioning him.

'Rhys Freeman wouldn't take the blame for him,' she said out loud. 'Especially when Father Godfrey practically accused him of treason.'

'Rhys Freeman might not know that Godfrey

took the cross,' Hereward pointed out. 'Don't forget, Uncle Owen said, "Ask the monk". He must have seen someone in robes in the chapel around the time he was attacked. It could just as easily have been a priest—like Father Godfrey.'

'But we know Rhys Freeman stole the bones,' Gwyneth objected. She heard Hereward sigh, as if he had given up hope of getting to sleep. 'It makes sense that he would have stolen the cross as well.'

'So where is it now?' Hereward spoke through a yawn.

'He sold it to Wasim Kharab.' As soon as she put words to her suspicions Gwyneth became more certain that she must be right. 'That would help Henry pay for men and weapons if he is planning another rebellion, even without the bones.'

'I liked Wasim,' said Hereward. 'I don't think he's a traitor.'

'It's not treason for him, is it?' Excitement surged through Gwyneth as she began to see how everything could fit together. She sat up, pushing back her thick blankets. 'Richard isn't his king.'

'Don't speak so loud,' Hereward warned her. 'Mother will hear you.'

Knowing he was right, Gwyneth forced herself to lie down again, though every muscle in her body wanted to leap up and go looking for Wasim Kharab then and there. 'It could have happened like that,' she whispered. 'You know it could.'

'Maybe.' Hereward yawned again. 'It still doesn't help us to get the cross back.'

'But it does! We saw Rhys Freeman loading boxes onto Wasim's cart. The cross must have been in one of them.'

'Then it's gone. Wasim left the village last night.'

'We could follow him. Hereward, if there's any hope that the cross is in that cart, we've *got* to follow him!'

'Better get Sheriff Thorson to do it,' said Hereward. 'If Wasim is working with Henry of Truro, some of Henry's men might be with him.'

'But Sheriff Thorson believed Master Freeman when he said he didn't steal the cross and he's furious with us because we listened at the window. He's making Ivo and Amabel do extra tasks in the house, and he said he would tell our parents if he caught us spying again. No, we've got to look for Wasim ourselves.'

The bed across the room creaked as Hereward turned over again. Gwyneth could just make out his humped shape underneath the blankets.

'All right,' he murmured. 'Anything you say. Tomorrow . . .'

The next day, Gwyneth and Hereward were not free to put their plan into action until they had taken the noon meal to the workmen at the abbey. The expected delivery of stone had still not arrived, so the work was making no progress. But there was better news of their uncle. Matt Green had visited him in the abbey infirmary. Owen Mason was conscious again, though very weak and confused, and he did not remember anything about the attack, not even the presence of the monk.

Two nights before, Wasim Kharab had left the village by the road leading towards the Tor. Gwyneth knew that if he had kept going he would be beyond their reach by now, but she could not help hoping that he had stopped to make camp, especially when the bad weather would have made travelling difficult. The rain had stopped but grey clouds still covered the sky, promising more to come. Mud spattered Hereward's boots and the hem of Gwyneth's skirt as they trudged away from the abbey gateway along the same road Wasim had taken.

As they left the last houses of the village behind them, they met Sim Short, a friend of their father's, knee-deep in water by the side of the road while he cut rushes for basket-making.

'Good morrow!' he called cheerfully. 'Where are you off to?'

'We're looking for the merchant, Wasim Kharab,' Gwyneth explained. 'Have you seen him?' When Master Short looked puzzled, she added hastily, 'Mother decided she should have bought more spices from him, so we said we'd try to find him.' She hoped fervently that God would forgive her for the lie—and that it would never come to Idony Mason's ears.

Master Short straightened up, one hand massaging his back, his reaping hook in the other. 'I saw him two nights ago, but not since,' he said. 'There's no use you looking for him. He'll be well away by now.'

'Well, we'll go a bit further,' Gwyneth replied. 'Thank you, Master Short!'

She could tell from Hereward's doubtful expression that he thought they were on a fool's errand, just like the basket-maker. But he didn't complain. Pushing aside her own doubts, Gwyneth led the way along the road, which had become a raised causeway across the flooded land on either side, with the wooded slopes of the Tor rising steeply out of a flat, grey expanse of water. Water birds sculled around in the reeds and ripples spread in circles where a fish had surfaced.

A dark speck on the shining water took shape as they drew near and Gwyneth saw a fisherman casting out his net from a coracle, a flimsy-looking wicker bowl covered with hides.

She waved to him; she had seen him selling his fish in the market-place, though she didn't know his name. The fisherman raised a hand in reply and dug a broad-bladed paddle into the water to drive his coracle closer to the road.

'Good morrow!' Gwyneth called. 'Have you seen Wasim Kharab?'

The fisherman shook his head. 'I don't know that name, young mistress.'

'A Moorish merchant,' Hereward explained. 'Wearing white robes. He would have been driving a big cart with a pair of mules.'

'Oh, him!' The fisherman grinned. 'I met him yesterday. His cart was mired in the mud and I helped him shift it—great heavy thing. I told him to make camp until the weather cleared, else he'd be stuck again.'

'And did he? Where?' Gwyneth asked eagerly.

The fisherman shrugged. 'Can't tell you that. But if he didn't, he's a fool.'

Gwyneth tugged Hereward's arm. 'Come on!'

She thanked the fisherman, who raised his paddle in farewell. Now she and Hereward moved on more quickly, spurred by hope. Very soon they came to a dip in the road where the mud had been churned up; they could still make out wheel tracks and the footprints of mules and men.

'This must be where he got stuck,' said Hereward. 'If he made camp, he might not be far away.'

As they went on, Gwyneth scanned the

ground for more tracks, but the rain had washed most of them away. Soon they came to a place where land appeared above the surface of the water, a tangle of brambles close to the road that gave way to shrubs and a few larger trees as the dry ground rose into a gentle hill. In one place the brambles had been pushed aside and trampled to allow something large to pass through them.

'That must be where he went!' said Gwyneth.

Hereward made a sign to her for silence and took the lead as they ventured along the path through the undergrowth that the mule cart had made. It forged almost straight ahead, then rounded a hawthorn thicket. Eagerly following her brother, Gwyneth bumped into him when he suddenly stopped. Looking over his shoulder she saw they had arrived at the edge of a clearing. Wasim Kharab's cart stood on the far side of a clump of hawthorn bushes. The mules had been unharnessed and tethered to a tree by long ropes that let them move around to graze. There was no sign of the merchant.

Hereward's eyes gleamed with excitement, though his voice was calm as he murmured, 'Now what do we do?'

Gwyneth felt her heart pounding. She realized that she had never truly believed that they would manage to overtake the merchant, only that she would never have forgiven herself if they had not tried. Now that she was faced with the cart, she was not sure what their next step should be.

The flap at the back of the covered cart was laced up, so they could see nothing of what was inside. Was Wasim in there, Gwyneth wondered, watching them to see what they would do next? The thought made her shiver.

'If he's here . . .' Her voice was shaky; she cleared her throat. 'We could ask him about the cross. He might not realize how important it is. If we explain to him, he might give it to us.'

Hereward raised his eyebrows, though he said nothing. Mustering her courage, Gwyneth advanced into the clearing until she stood close to the cart. 'Master Kharab, are you there?' she called.

Silence. Hereward came up to join her, and she called again, but there was still no reply.

Gwyneth flashed a swift glance at her brother. 'I don't think he's in there.' She took another step towards the cart.

'Gwyneth!' There was a warning in

Hereward's voice. 'You're mad if you're thinking of searching. What if he comes back—and what about that snake?'

Gwyneth flinched. Then she thought of turning round and going home again with their mission unaccomplished.

'I don't care,' she said. 'This might be our one chance of finding the cross.' She hurried forward and began unfastening the lacing on the flap. 'You keep watch.'

Still moving as quietly as she could, she let down the backboard of the cart, pulled aside the flap, and climbed in. Straightening up, she could not restrain a gasp of surprise. It was like stepping into another world.

The canvas roof was high enough for her to stand comfortably upright. Silken hangings were draped between the supports and beneath the roof of the cart—rose-coloured, deep crimson, and jade green, embroidered with gold and silver thread. A silver lamp hung from one of the beams. The floor was spread with rugs woven in elaborate designs of flowers and leaves. The air was filled with a smell like the incense the abbey monks burnt at Mass, though stronger and spicier.

At one side of the cart was a heap of cushions and a fur bedcover, which must be where Wasim Kharab slept. At the other side were chests of carved wood with silver locks and hinges. More boxes were piled up at the other end of the cart, and from their size and shape Gwyneth recognized the ones that came from Rhys Freeman. Two or three bundles were heaped up beside them.

Gwyneth crept forward, alert all the time for movement that might warn her of the presence of the snake. She spotted the basket she had seen in the market-place, half hidden at the head of Wasim Kharab's bed, but dared not lift the lid to find out whether the snake was inside.

When she prodded the bundles, they felt soft as if they contained some kind of fabric. Certainly there was nothing in there big enough to be a solid metal cross two handspans long. Opening the lid of the box on top of the pile, she found more of the small boxes containing scraps of bone, like the ones she and Hereward had discovered in Rhys Freeman's cellar.

Gwyneth closed the box again and tried to lift it so that she could search the one underneath, but it was too heavy for her to move. Creeping back to the opening she stuck her head out and saw Hereward with his back to her, shifting uneasily from foot to foot.

'Hereward!' she whispered. Her brother jumped and spun round as if he thought Wasim Kharab had sneaked up on him from behind.

'I need your help,' Gwyneth hissed. 'Hurry!'

With a last glance around the clearing, Hereward climbed up into the cart beside her. Together they had no difficulty in moving the boxes and searching them, but to their disappointment they discovered that all they held were Rhys Freeman's fake holy relics: boxes of bones and nails and enough scraps of net to catch all the fish in the Sea of Galilee. The cross with the inscription was not there.

'Here, then,' Gwyneth said, abandoning the last box to fling open the nearest of Wasim Kharab's storage chests. That one contained spices; the next, more of the sticky sweetmeats he had given them in the marketplace. The third held bolts of silk and a fourth the embroidery threads Marion le Fevre had admired. There was nowhere the cross could be hidden.

Gwyneth sat back in frustration while Hereward investigated the bedding and felt carefully around the silk hangings.

'It isn't here,' he said.

Gwyneth was reluctant to admit defeat, but she had to agree with her brother. 'We'd better go,' she whispered, but just at that moment she heard the sound of a soft footfall outside.

She and Hereward stared at each other in alarm. They just had time to close the last box and heave it back into its place on the pile before the flap of the cart was pulled back.

Wasim Kharab was standing there with a look of faint surprise on his face. At the same moment, Gwyneth discovered where the snake had been all this time. A soft hissing came from the folds of the merchant's robes, and the reptile stretched out its head towards Gwyneth and Hereward. Its eyes glittered and its forked tongue flickered back and forth.

'Well,' said Wasim Kharab. 'To what do I owe this pleasure?'

Chapter Eleven

Gwyneth felt as if the silence was stretching out for ever. She didn't dare try to push past Wasim Kharab and run, not while he was holding the snake. Her throat felt dry with terror.

'We . . . we're sorry,' she stammered. 'We saw the cart, and we . . .'

Wasim smiled, his teeth white against the copper of his skin. 'Perhaps you wished for more sweetmeats, yes?' he suggested. His voice was soft, but to Gwyneth it sounded as menacing as the hissing of the snake.

'Yes, that . . . that would be wonderful,' she managed to reply, not sure if the merchant was offering to give them some of the sweetmeats or if he was about to accuse them of trying to steal them.

'And we'd like to see some more magic, if you please.' Hereward tried to sound confident, but Gwyneth heard a betraying quiver in his voice.

'Magic? Of course.' Gwyneth jumped nervously as Wasim Kharab reached out one long-fingered coppery hand and seemed to pluck a silken ribbon out of the air. He presented it to her with a flourish. 'For your hair, young mistress.'

'Th-thank you.' Gwyneth's fear began to ebb, to be replaced by guilt. It couldn't be right to take a gift from the merchant when they had entered his cart uninvited and searched all his possessions.

'And for you, my young friend,' Wasim said to Hereward, 'perhaps this . . .' He closed his empty hand into a fist and opened it to reveal a tiny model of a horse, carved out of bone.

Hereward reached out hesitantly to take it, one eye on the snake. Wasim laughed and stroked one hand down the iridescent black scales. 'Don't be afraid of Yasmin, my friends. She is quite harmless, I assure you.'

Gwyneth was not sure she believed him, but she forced herself to smile. She began wondering what would be the best way to say goodbye to the merchant and make their escape when she saw that his gaze had fallen on the pile of boxes at the far end of the cart. The last one, which they had put away so quickly, was out of line with the others, and its lid had not been replaced properly.

Wasim's eyebrows lifted slightly. 'Did you come here searching for relics? They are very popular with all my customers,' he said.

'But how do you know they're real?' Gwyneth blurted out.

She caught a warning glance from Hereward and instantly regretted her words. Master Kharab might easily take offence, and he still held the snake.

The merchant's voice was as silken as ever. 'I bought them in good faith,' he said, his calm brown eyes fixed on Gwyneth. 'Who am I to judge if this thing or that is as old as people want to believe? Surely it is the comfort which such relics bring that is important?'

'Yes—I'm sure you're right,' Gwyneth said desperately. 'And now I really think we must be going . . .'

'Without your sweetmeats?' Wasim lifted the snake Yasmin to coil around his shoulders while he opened the chest.

Gwyneth took a step back. 'N-no, I thank you, sir. We have to go.'

'Our mother will be looking for us,' Hereward added.

Wasim straightened up and gestured towards the opening at the back of the cart. 'Then farewell, my friends,' he said. 'May you go in peace. We will meet again, I'm sure.'

Hereward bobbed his head and replied, 'Yes, I'm sure we will,' while Gwyneth muttered a hasty goodbye.

She had never been so relieved in her life as when they climbed out of the cart and hurried across the clearing and back to the road. Her heart was beating hard and her breath came short as if she had been running.

'I'm sorry,' she said to Hereward. 'It's my fault he caught us.'

Hereward shrugged. 'At least he wasn't angry.'

'Do you think he knows those relics are fake?' Gwyneth asked.

'I don't know.' Her brother frowned. 'What matters is that he hasn't got the cross. I can't see where else it could have been in that cart.'

They trudged along in silence for a while. 'It

looks as if Rhys Freeman was telling the truth when he said he didn't take it,' Gwyneth said at last. 'And if he told the truth about what he stole, maybe he told the truth when he said he saw someone throw a bundle into the water near his eel traps. That could have been the cross.'

'We've already looked there,' Hereward pointed out.

'But we didn't look for long. The hermit came, and you fell in the river.'

'Yes . . .' Hereward was thoughtful. 'Gwyneth, we've never asked ourselves *why* the hermit was there that day. Suppose *he* threw the cross into the river and then came back to search for it?'

Gwyneth halted and faced her brother, remembering her fears when she first saw the hermit by the river, when Hereward got his foot stuck. But would he have rescued Hereward from the eel trap and healed his ankle if he had been there for some other dark purpose?

'Uncle Owen could easily have mistaken him for a monk,' Hereward went on excitedly, walking faster so that Gwyneth had to set off again, almost running, to keep up with him. 'The light was bad in the chapel. His brown robe could have looked black.'

Gwyneth's mind was whirling. She had begun to think of the hermit as a friend, but she had to admit that Hereward could be right. 'Then we ought to search again,' she decided. 'He might not have found the cross when he went back to look for it—after all, we didn't see it. Or maybe we ought to look for his cell and see if it's there.'

By now they were following the road that led alongside the Tor, not far from the place where Rhys Freeman said he had seen the cloaked figure. Though the afternoon was wearing on, there was still enough light left for a search. Gwyneth remembered the tasks that would be waiting for them back at the Crown, and then pushed them to the back of her mind. This was more important.

By the time they came to the path that led across marshy ground to the river, Gwyneth was beginning to feel desperate. If they didn't find the cross soon, she thought, it might pass out of their reach forever. No one would believe the bones belonged to King Arthur and Queen

Guinevere, and the abbey and the village would still be poor.

The marshes were wetter than ever after the heavy rain, and in some places Gwyneth and Hereward had to wade. Gwyneth raised her skirt to the knee and tucked the folds into her girdle to keep them dry.

She quickened her pace when she heard the soft running of the river ahead of them, only to come to a halt as she rounded a clump of osiers and reached the place where Rhys Freeman set his eel traps.

Seated on the fallen tree trunk was a familiar brown-robed figure.

Chapter Twelve

Gwyneth froze. She was stunned to see the hermit again, so soon after she and Hereward had just been discussing him. Could it really be true that he had stolen the cross? Had he come back to search for it again? Gwyneth realized uncomfortably that she and her brother knew nothing about him, and were alone with him in this remote place.

She took Hereward by the arm and began to back away. At the same moment the hermit raised his brows with a look of enquiry and pointed to Hereward's ankle.

'Y-yes, it's better,' Hereward stammered. 'There's not even a scar.'

The hermit smiled, and his face seemed so kind that Gwyneth felt foolish for suspecting him of such dark crimes. She was about to ask him if he had seen anything of the cross when he rose to his feet and began to move away in the direction of the Tor. Gwyneth's question died on her lips, and her heart began thumping wildly as the hermit glanced over his shoulder and beckoned for them to follow him.

Gwyneth stood frozen, clutching her brother's arm. When the hermit reached the nearest trees, he turned back and beckoned again. Hereward took a step towards him.

'Wait,' Gwyneth whispered, for once more cautious than her brother. 'We'd be mad to follow him.'

'But what if he can tell us something?' said Hereward. 'If he can't speak, maybe he has to show us.'

As the hermit beckoned a third time, Hereward shook off his sister's hand and set off after him, his feet squelching through puddles in his haste to catch up. Gwyneth hesitated briefly, but she could not let him go alone. Pushing down her fears, she followed.

The hermit led them along a path that wound through thorn trees to the lower slopes of the Tor.

'Do you think this leads to his cell?' Hereward murmured.

'I don't know.' Gwyneth managed to keep her voice steady. 'He could be taking us anywhere.'

'I don't think he'll hurt us.' Gwyneth thought Hereward was trying to convince himself as much as her. 'He healed my ankle.'

Somehow Gwyneth found that was not much comfort now.

The path began to climb more steeply, and at last they came out onto open ground. Glancing back, Gwyneth saw the grey walls of the abbey below her with the houses of the village clustered around. Smoke from hearth fires was rising into the still air. Everything looked peaceful and safe, and Gwyneth wished fervently that she was back there.

Just above them a twisted thorn tree bent over a thicket of brambles. A smooth, rounded stone rose out of the tangled stems, looking like an enormous egg half buried in the ground. Picking up a dead branch, the hermit drew back the curtain of brambles to reveal a hole just big enough for someone to squeeze inside.

Then he beckoned again and pointed into the gap.

'You want us to go in there?' Hereward's voice was higher-pitched than usual; Gwyneth shared his wariness about going into that small, dark space.

The hermit did not speak, but let the bramble curtain fall and opened the pouch at his girdle. From it he took flint and steel, and a rush taper in a wooden holder. Striking a spark, he lit the taper and held it out to Gwyneth.

The offer of a light calmed her, and the hermit's reassuring smile revived her confidence further. It seemed less likely that the hermit meant them any harm if he was sharing his precious light with them, and she could bear the thought of the hole in the hill now that she knew she would not be facing it in the dark.

'I'll go,' she said softly to her brother. 'You run and tell father where I've gone. Fetch help.'

'No.' Hereward's face was stubborn. 'If you're going, I'm coming with you.' He echoed Gwyneth's thoughts. 'The hermit's giving us a light, and he did heal my ankle. Why should he want to hurt us now?'

'Come on, then.' Gwyneth climbed up the slope and took the taper from the hermit. Ducking her head, she managed to wriggle through the brambles and heard Hereward coming up behind her.

At first she could see nothing but blackness beyond the wavering circle of light cast by the taper, but once she had shuffled forward a few steps to let Hereward enter more light leaked in and showed them a tunnel leading downwards into the heart of the Tor.

The hermit had not followed them, though Gwyneth thought she could hear him moving around outside.

'Why has he brought us here?' Hereward asked, peering round his sister.

Gwyneth hesitated. All her instincts were telling her to turn round and scramble out. Perhaps the hermit wanted to trap them. Perhaps he would bring a stone and roll it over the gap, so that they could not get out, and no one would ever find them. Panic beat in her throat.

Then she took a breath and forced herself to be calm. She could not believe that the hermit was an evil man. Everything she had seen of him told her that he was kind and gentle. Besides, curiosity was urging her on. All her life Gwyneth had heard rumours that the Tor was hollow, but she had never managed to find a way in until now.

'There's something he wants to show us,' she said out loud. 'We have to go on.'

She began to walk along the tunnel. There was enough light from the taper to show her the steep downward slope, the floor rough with loose stones. The walls and roof were tight-packed soil, with roots writhing in and out. After the first few steps it grew wider, though Gwyneth could still touch both walls with her outstretched hands.

The light from the entrance quickly faded behind them, and it was not long before she could see nothing but shadows crowding round the feeble glow from the taper. Gwyneth's renewed courage threatened to desert her, and putting one foot in front of the other was the hardest thing she had ever done.

Gradually the tunnel levelled out; they were still going down, but only very gently now. The packed soil of the tunnel walls gave way to rock slick with water. Steadying herself against it, Gwyneth almost stumbled when suddenly her hand met nothing. A gust of colder air washed over them from a side passage and the taper flickered. Gwyneth froze, cautiously reaching up with her hand to shelter the flame until it steadied again.

'Which way?' she murmured, hardly daring

to breathe in case the light went out and left them in a darkness that was blacker than night.

'Keep on going down.' Hereward's voice was tense. 'That looks like the main tunnel.'

Carefully shielding the taper, Gwyneth walked on. She could hear the trickle of running water, and a moment later the flame in her hand was reflected in the black surface of a stream.

'Be careful,' Gwyneth warned, stepping cautiously into it. The water was icy cold.

The stream grew deeper until it covered her ankles; at the same time her head scraped against the roof and she had to stoop. Her heart thudded as she wondered what they would do if the water rose until it filled the tunnel, but to her relief it soon grew shallower, and she stepped out onto dry ground again.

The tunnel roof grew lower still until Gwyneth was almost bent double, but the floor was smooth and even. She heard the rushing of water somewhere ahead—the sound of a river, not the shallow stream they had just forded. Her pace grew slower as she tested the ground in front of her before she dared to take a step.

Suddenly Gwyneth realized that the impenetrable blackness beyond the light of the flame was lifting; and she could make out the faint outline of the tunnel ahead.

'Daylight!'

'Are we coming out?' Hereward sounded hopeful.

'We're coming to somewhere.'

The light grew stronger as the tunnel ended abruptly and Gwyneth was able to stand upright again. She stepped forward to let Hereward out and looked around, her eyes stinging in what seemed at first to be brilliant light.

They were standing in a vast chamber hollowed out of the rock. Pale daylight filtered through a couple of narrow cracks high above her head. Spears of stone pointed downwards from the roof, while others rose to meet them from the floor of the cave. Here and there they met and became pillars, so that Gwyneth felt as if she was standing in the middle of a vast church, bigger even than the new abbey church the masons were building.

She and Hereward had emerged on a slippery outcrop of rock just above a river of fast-moving dark water. It hugged the far side of the cavern, edged on both sides by spiky black rocks. Branches and tussocks of grass were borne along in the flood, swept down from the outside world.

Gwyneth and Hereward clambered down from the outcrop to the floor of the cave. About halfway across the cave the river poured over a precipice of broken rock into a foaming pool, to vanish a little further on through a dark hole in the chamber wall.

'What do we do now?' Hereward had to shout to make himself heard above the roar of the water.

'I don't know,' Gwyneth shouted back.

She began to retrace her steps along the river. She had almost reached the mouth of the tunnel they came in by when Hereward clutched her arm. He was pointing urgently to something on the other side of the river.

'There—between those rocks!'

Gwyneth gazed, puzzled, across the surging water. At first she couldn't tell what Hereward was getting so excited about. Then she saw it.

Lodged between two rocks, just above water level, was a bundle two or three handspans long wrapped in rough sacking and fastened with cord. A pale glint of metal showed where something poked out from between the folds.

'It must be the cross!' said Hereward. 'I'm going to get it.'

'Wait! You can't!'

Gwyneth made a grab for her brother's arm, but Hereward was too quick for her. Scrambling up to the top of the outcrop he balanced briefly on its very edge and then leapt for the far side of the river. Gwyneth bit back a scream as she imagined him falling short and being swept away, or going too far and slamming into the rock wall. She screwed her eyes tight shut and felt her nails dig into her palms.

When she opened her eyes again Hereward had landed safely on the narrow ledge between the water and the wall. Carefully he began to edge his way downstream until he came to the bundle. He lay flat on the rocks above, stretching down, but the cross—if it was the cross—was still out of reach. With scarcely a pause, Hereward swung himself down into the current. Water surged around his shoulders, but he managed to pull himself along until he reached the bundle. Hanging on precariously with one hand, he grasped the sacking with the other and thrust the bundle down the front of his tunic.

Gwyneth could hardly breathe. Her brother had succeeded in retrieving the bundle, but how was he going to get back? He could never leap up to the outcrop, and the river was flowing so fast that he would be swept away if he tried to swim.

'Climb out! Stay on that side!' she shouted. 'I'll go for help!'

She thought Hereward had heard her. He began pulling himself out of the river again, but suddenly his fingers slipped. He fell back, scrabbling vainly at the smooth surface of the rock. His cry of alarm was swiftly drowned by the noise of the river as the water boiled around him.

'No!' Gwyneth cried.

She stared helplessly as the current swept Hereward out into midstream. His head went under and then resurfaced. The force of the water was too strong for him, and he was swept helplessly downstream to the waterfall and the gaping black nothingness beyond.

Chapter Thirteen

Gwyneth set down the taper and ran alongside the river, keeping pace with her brother. Hereward's white face bobbed in the current. He was managing to stay afloat, but it would not be long before he would be carried down into the heart of the hill.

Gwyneth flung herself down the rocky precipice, catching a horrified glimpse of her brother as he was swept over the waterfall in a tangle of limbs. A loose stone slipped under her feet and she fell the rest of the way, jarring every bone in her body.

She scrambled to her knees in time to see Hereward fight his way to the surface in the foaming pool below the falls. A tongue of rock jutted out where the river poured over the lip of the pool. Stumbling in her haste, Gwyneth ventured out to the very end of it and knelt there with a hand outstretched to grab Hereward as he was carried past.

In despair she realized that she could not reach far enough. Without hesitating she slid into the water, feeling the current tug at her as the river bottom shelved steeply. Gripping the rock with one hand, she stretched the other towards her brother.

'Hereward! Here!' she shouted.

Hereward looked exhausted but he was still trying to swim, his hands reaching out as he was swept down towards her. Gwyneth did not dare turn to look at the yawning darkness behind her, but she pictured it in her mind like a mouth ready to swallow them both.

An eddy in the water brought Hereward towards her. His fingers brushed hers; his arms thrashed, and at last Gwyneth was able to grasp his wrist and pull him closer to the bank.

When he had found his feet she gave him a push, helping him to climb over the rocks to the safety of the cave floor, then clambered up after him to collapse panting by his side.

For a long time they could do nothing but lie there, soaked and shivering, with the roar of the river in their ears. At last Gwyneth sat up and began wringing water out of her skirt. The light in the cave was growing dimmer, and she realized that outside the short autumn day must be drawing to an end.

'Come on.' She shook her brother's shoulder. 'We must be getting back.'

Hereward sat up. 'I thought I was going to die.' He cast one quick glance at the gaping hole where the river disappeared, then looked away again. 'Thank you.'

Gwyneth forced a smile. 'And what would I have told mother and father if you hadn't come back?'

'Well, let's see if my dip was worth it.' Hereward hauled the sodden bundle out of the front of his tunic and Gwyneth felt her heart pound as his shaking fingers fumbled with the knot of the cord.

The folds of sacking fell away to reveal the lead cross with the inscription that proved the bones that had been found in the abbey grounds were truly those of King Arthur and Queen Guinevere.

Gwyneth let out a long sigh. 'We've found it!'

In spite of his exhaustion, Hereward's eyes

shone. 'Now the pilgrims will come back,' he murmured.

'We must take it back to the abbey right away.' Rising to her feet, Gwyneth pulled Hereward up beside her and headed for the passage they had come in by. The taper was still alight where she had left it, though it was burning low, and she was afraid it would not last. She was not sure she could find her way through the tunnels in complete darkness.

This time she felt so weary that the passage seemed to go on for ever. The taper guttered, and for all Gwyneth's care in shielding it the flame sank to a tiny glowing bead and then died altogether. Fear pulsed through Gwyneth until she realized that she could see a faint light filtering from somewhere ahead.

'We're almost there!' she gasped.

A few steps more, and she and Hereward squeezed through the gap again and stood on the slopes of the Tor. Gwyneth took a long breath of the cool, damp air. At first she thought the hermit had gone and her fears returned. Had he abandoned them to whatever perils lay beneath the Tor, she wondered, never expecting that they would come out of the tunnel safely?

Then she heard the crackling of flames and turned to see that not far away, under the thorn tree, a fire had been kindled. The hermit was sitting beside it, feeding it with sticks.

Bright flames lit up the man's face as he turned to them. 'Did you find it?'

Gwyneth stared in amazement. The hermit could speak!

'I am not under a vow,' he said as if he could read her mind. 'But I only speak when I have something of worth to say.'

'Then . . . will you tell us who you are?' Gwyneth asked. 'What is your name?'

The hermit hesitated. At last he said, 'You may call me Ursus.' He beckoned them both over to the fire and repeated, 'Did you find it?'

Gwyneth glanced at her brother. Had the hermit known that the cross was there all along? And how could he have known they had been searching for it? All her suspicions came crowding back, but they were quickly followed by the thought that if the hermit had stolen the cross, he surely wouldn't have shown them where it was.

Hereward had clearly decided to trust the man. Pulling the cross from his tunic again, he walked over to Ursus and held it out. 'We found this.'

'And Hereward almost died for it!' Gwyneth exclaimed, her fear spilling over into a burst of anger.

'But he did not drown,' Ursus replied. 'You have both come back safely, with the treasure that will restore your abbey and your home.'

'Yes, Arthur's cross,' said Hereward, hugging it to him. Curiously, he added, 'Did you know it was there?'

'Know?' Ursus's eyes were dark and secret, fixed on the flames. 'I know little. Only this—that there is always a time for things to be found.' He looked up at Gwyneth and smiled at her with great kindness. Reaching out, he dug strong brown fingers into the rich leaf-mould and gently uncovered a sleeping acorn.

'See? Nothing is lost for ever,' he said. 'Even though what you seek may be hidden for a while.'

Gwyneth's whole body ached with exhaustion as she and Hereward made their way back through the marshes. Her brother must be wearier still, she realized, after that struggle in the river. But they were both borne up by the triumph of knowing that they had found the cross that confirmed the identity of the bones, and would secure the future of the whole village.

'We'll go straight to the abbey,' she said.

As they were passing the place where Rhys Freeman set his eel traps, Gwyneth heard the sound of footsteps splashing through the pools, and spotted someone moving around near the river bank. Wondering if Osbert Teller might be inspecting the traps, she drew Hereward into the shelter of a clump of osiers. Then she saw that the man by the river was Brother Peter.

The elderly monk was stumbling along the waterside, poking a staff into hollows and clumps of reeds, and muttering, 'I can't find it . . . I can't find it.'

Gwyneth felt a surge of compassion for the frail monk. He should not be wandering around in the cold and damp as darkness fell. Whatever was he doing so far from the abbey?

'Brother Peter, what's the matter? Can we help you?'

The monk peered at Gwyneth and seemed

to recognize her, or at least to realize that she was no threat. 'No . . . no,' he murmured vaguely, and repeated, 'I can't find it.'

'Tell us what you've lost, and we'll help you look,' said Hereward.

For some reason his offer seemed to alarm Brother Peter even more. 'I can't—I can't tell anyone. And it's lost for ever . . .'

Gently Gwyneth took his arm. 'Let's go home,' she said. 'If you tell Abbot Henry what's troubling you, I'm sure he'll be able to help.'

Brother Peter shook his head, but he did not try to resist as Gwyneth led him back along the path towards the village. Hereward brought up the rear, leaving the darkening marshes to the waterbirds and fishes, and to the mysterious hermit Ursus.

Chapter Fourteen

Darkness had fallen by the time they reached the abbey. As Gwyneth and Hereward led Brother Peter through the arched gateway they heard the bell begin to toll for vespers and saw a procession of dark-robed monks approaching the doors of the Lady Chapel. Brother Barnabas was in the lead, carrying a lantern, followed closely by Abbot Henry and Godfrey de Massard.

Leaving Brother Peter to follow at his own pace, Gwyneth and Hereward ran across the grass and came up with the monks as they were about to enter the chapel.

'What is this?' Godfrey de Massard was the first to speak, his voice and his expression severe. 'What are you children doing here, interrupting our services? Get you home at once.'

'Abbot Henry, we *must* speak to you!' Gwyneth panted, ignoring Father Godfrey.

'We've something important to show you.'

The priest from Wells opened his mouth for a stinging rebuke, but Abbot Henry silenced him with a lifted hand. 'What is it, my child?' he asked.

For answer, Hereward hauled the bundle out of his tunic, and Gwyneth folded back the wrappings to reveal the cross. Abbot Henry's eyes widened and a gasp of wonder rose from the monks, who gathered round eagerly, their eyes shining in the light from the lantern. They stretched out their hands to touch the relic as if they could scarcely believe it had returned to them.

Reverently Abbot Henry took it from Gwyneth's hands and held it aloft. 'Lord God, we thank you,' he intoned in a voice that sounded too strong for his slight, scholarly body. 'For you have restored our treasure to us.'

Gwyneth just had time to notice the look of disbelief on the face of Godfrey de Massard before a quavering voice sounded behind her and she looked round to see Brother Peter staring in dismay at the cross.

'No! No!' he cried. 'It cannot be! Now King Arthur will never lie quiet.'

Gwyneth was astonished. Hereward was quicker to understand what was upsetting the elderly Peter.

'It was the cross you were looking for in the marshes!' he exclaimed. More quietly, he added, 'Brother Peter, tell us what grieves you so.'

'Yes, Brother.' Abbot Henry handed the cross to Father Godfrey, who looked as if the abbot had offered him a dead rat, then stepped forward until he faced Brother Peter and rested a gentle hand on his shoulder. 'I know something has been troubling you these past days. As your abbot I beg you to tell me and be at peace.'

Trembling, the old monk looked up into Abbot Henry's eyes. 'It was I who took the cross,' he confessed.

Gwyneth stared at the old man in astonishment. She could hardly believe that after all their suspicions, the real thief was someone she and Hereward had never even considered. She remembered how upset Brother Peter had been when the bones were first uncovered, and how in Rhys Freeman's cellar he had tried to persuade Brother Barnabas that the shopkeeper had not stolen the cross as well as the bones. Gwyneth guessed that the old monk had not wanted Master Freeman to be blamed for the crime he himself had committed.

With a glance Abbot Henry silenced the excited murmuring that had broken out among the monks. 'Go on,' he said encouragingly.

'I went to the chapel before prime that morning and found Master Mason lying injured,' Brother Peter explained quietly. 'The bones had gone from the oaken coffin, but the cross was still on the altar. I took it because—'

'And left Uncle Owen lying there!' Gwyneth couldn't help bursting out. The injured man must have seen Brother Peter pass by, which is why he told them to 'ask the monk'.

Brother Peter glanced at her, shaking his head in confusion. 'I know, I know. I have never committed so grievous a sin in all my life.'

'Tell us why you did it,' Abbot Henry prompted gently.

'Already there had been so much argument about the bones,' said Brother Peter, his voice quivering. 'I could not believe so much dissent was God's will! I thought that if the cross was gone and no one could prove the bones were Arthur's, then all would be forgotten, and if the bones were recovered they could be buried again and lie in peace. I—I hid the cross near the gate, and then I went to find Brother Padraig to get his help for Master Mason, but by then all had been discovered. So then I—'

'You took the cross into the marshes and threw it into the river!' Hereward realized out loud.

'Yes . . . yes.'

'So Rhys Freeman was telling the truth,' said Gwyneth.

'I sinned again,' admitted the old monk. 'I let Master Freeman be suspected of stealing the cross as well as the bones.' He shook his head despairingly. 'Can I ever be forgiven?'

'Lose no sleep over Rhys Freeman.' Father Godfrey spoke up, and to Gwyneth's surprise his voice was curt but not unsympathetic. 'He has sins enough of his own to pay for.'

'God's forgiveness is for all,' Abbot Henry assured Brother Peter. 'Come into the chapel now. I think a penance of a hundred Hail Marys will suffice—do you agree, Father Godfrey?'

Godfrey de Massard gave a brusque nod. Tears

overflowed from Brother Peter's eyes, and he covered his face with his hands. Brother Padraig emerged from the crowd of monks behind the abbot, put an arm round the old man's shoulders and led him gently into the chapel.

'Now,' said Abbot Henry, looking at Gwyneth and Hereward. 'Tell us how you came to find the cross.'

Gwyneth paused. There was such a long story to tell, as tangled as the thorns around the Tor, and filled with the mystery of the hermit Ursus and of the Tor itself. Gwyneth was still not sure that she understood exactly how she and her brother had been led to the cross, so how could she possibly explain it to Abbot Henry? She could only think that Ursus had seen Brother Peter throwing the cross into the water and had worked out that the swollen river would wash it under the Tor; but something warned her that the hermit would not welcome being sought out as a witness to the frail monk's misguided actions.

'We searched the passages underneath the Tor,' she said at last, hoping that the abbot would not ask too many probing questions. 'The river had carried it far underground.'

Abbot Henry's eyes grew wide with wonder, and even Father Godfrey looked reluctantly impressed.

'Then you showed great courage,' said Abbot Henry. 'And God was truly with you. The abbey will reward you, but for now, get you home quickly. Your clothes are wet and the night grows chill. No doubt your mother will wonder where you are.'

'Yes, Father Abbot.' Hereward bowed to Abbot Henry, and Gwyneth dropped a curtsy.

A pang of guilt shot through her as she remembered all the tasks at home that they had left undone. Yet she knew her mother and father would not be angry when they heard the story of how they had found the cross, and she felt a warm feeling of triumph. Glancing at Hereward, she saw from his shining eyes that he shared it too.

The abbot stretched out a hand in a sign of blessing, and then he and the rest of the monks withdrew into the chapel. Only Brother Timothy hung back. To Gwyneth's surprise he looked as if something was troubling him.

'How did you know where to look for the cross?' he asked curiously.

Gwyneth looked at him for a moment, then decided to tell the truth. At least one of the monks deserved to know they had an unexpected ally. 'A hermit told us,' she replied. 'His name is Ursus. Do you know him?'

Brother Timothy hesitated before shaking his head. 'I know of no Ursus, but I should like to meet him.'

'We could take you,' Hereward offered.

'Thank you,' said the young monk. The sound of chanting arose from inside the chapel as the service of vespers began. 'If Abbot Henry gives me leave, I'll meet you outside the gates after prime tomorrow.'

When Hereward and Gwyneth set out to meet Brother Timothy next morning, they heard shouting and laughter coming from the market-place.

Hereward flashed a grin at his sister. 'Word must have spread that the cross has been found.'

But he was wrong. When they turned the corner into the market-place Gwyneth was amazed to see that the stocks had been set up in the middle. Rhys Freeman was sitting with his legs trapped between the wooden beams while a jeering crowd of villagers surrounded him and pelted him with rubbish.

On the other side of the market-place his shop was shut up, the shutters firmly barred. Gwyneth wasn't surprised; news had already come to the Crown that Osbert Teller had left the village for good.

The Thorson twins pushed their way out of the crowd, their red hair in disarray and their cheeks flushed. Ivo Thorson grabbed Hereward and thrust a rotting apple into his hand. 'Father sentenced him!' he announced. 'And he's lucky not to hang.'

Amabel delved into the bag at her feet for another apple which she hurled at the wretched shopkeeper. It burst in the very centre of his forehead, and the brown pulp dripped into his eyes and mouth.

'That's for stealing our basket!' Amabel yelled.

Rhys Freeman spat out the pulp. 'Young limb of Satan! Wait till I get hold of you!'

Gwyneth might have felt sorry for him if he hadn't been shouting and cursing at all the villagers, promising what he would do when he was free. As it was, he didn't seem to have learnt his lesson at all, and she guessed there would be more trouble with him in the future.

'Finn Thorson fined him, too.' A familiar voice spoke behind her and she turned to see the lanky figure of Brother Timothy. 'Abbot Henry will use the money to help the poorest of the villagers.'

Gwyneth nodded, pleased to hear that; losing money might be more of a punishment for the greedy shopkeeper than the humiliation of the stocks.

'There's to be a special service in the abbey to celebrate the recovery of the bones and the cross,' Brother Timothy went on, a joyful smile lighting up his face. 'God has greatly blessed us. This morning a messenger came to Lord Ralph FitzStephen to say that a load of stone is coming upriver and will be here tomorrow.'

'So the masons can start work again!' Hereward looked pleased. 'Everything's going to come right at last.'

'And we have the two of you to thank for it,' said Brother Timothy.

Embarrassed by his praise, Gwyneth glanced away and spotted Marion le Fevre standing on the edge of the crowd. She was watching the villagers pelting Rhys Freeman, though she did not join in.

Gwyneth went over and bobbed a curtsy. 'Good day, mistress. Have you heard the news?'

Emerald green eyes turned to look at her. 'News? About Master Freeman?'

'No, about the cross. We found it yesterday, in a stream under the Tor!'

Marion le Fevre's eyes flew wide in astonishment and for a moment Gwyneth thought she saw a flash of darkness there. 'Under the Tor!' she exclaimed. 'However did you think to look there?'

'A hermit showed us,' said Gwyneth. 'His name is Ursus.'

Marion le Fevre frowned. 'Ursus . . .' she mused. 'And where did you meet this Ursus, child?'

'By the river. He healed Hereward's ankle.'

'I should like to see him,' said the embroideress, and added, 'He must be a very holy man.'

'Oh, yes, mistress, I'm sure he is. And you have seen him—do you remember, he was there in the market, the day Wasim Kharab came? A tall man in a brown robe.'

Marion le Fevre shook her head. 'I don't remember.' A moment later her musical laugh rang out. 'It's of no importance. Not like your news about the cross—that is truly wonderful!'

Before Gwyneth could reply, she was distracted by Hereward tugging at her sleeve. 'Come on,' he said. 'We haven't time to stand here. Brother Timothy's waiting.'

He took aim and let fly with the apple Ivo had given him and grinned with satisfaction as it struck Rhys Freeman full in the face. 'He looks like the boar's head at Christmastide, with an apple in its mouth,' he declared.

Waving goodbye to Mistress le Fevre and the twins, Gwyneth and Hereward headed towards the Tor with Brother Timothy. Hereward led the way confidently through the tangle of thorns and undergrowth, back to the place the hermit had shown them the day before. Eventually they came out to the smooth stone that rose from the bramble thicket, with the thorn tree overhanging it.

'This is the place,' said Gwyneth.

'But where is the passage?' Brother Timothy asked.

Gwyneth stared. There was no sign of a tunnel entrance beside the stone. Hereward picked up a fallen branch and stabbed it into the brambles, trying to find the place where Ursus had drawn back the curtain of stems.

Gwyneth listened in growing confusion to the end of the branch thudding on hard ground. 'I don't understand! This *must be* the right place. Look, here's the fire that Ursus made.'

She jabbed the toe of her shoe into the feathery, burnt-out ash where the hermit had lit his fire as if it could reveal the answer to the puzzle. A single unburnt acorn rolled out of the cinders, scraps of earth still clinging to it.

Hereward came to join her. He bent down and picked up the acorn, thoughtfully brushing the earth away, and stowed it in his belt pouch.

'There's always a time for things to be found,' he said, echoing the words of the hermit.

'But we can *never* find Ursus.'

Gwyneth stopped. Just a few days ago, it had seemed as if the cross and the bones of Arthur were lost for ever; but thanks to Ivo's mischief with the flooded cellar, and the hermit guiding her and Hereward to the underground cavern, the relics had been returned to the abbey where they belonged. Only Ursus was missing from the celebrations. Gwyneth flashed an apologetic look at Brother Timothy. 'People will start to think we made him up. But I promise he does exist, and without him we'd never have found the cross.'

The young monk smiled, kindness illuminating his bony features so that for a moment Gwyneth was struck by his likeness to the hermit.

'Don't worry,' said Brother Timothy. 'I believe that you saw him and spoke with him, just as you said. And I believe that when the time is right, just as for the acorn, you will see him again.'